~~Recieve~~ ~~Abandon~~ All Hope, All Ye Who Enter Here

Imagine, if you will, there was a Gospel According to Stephen King or Neil Gaiman, the masters of horror and the macabre. Heretical? Blasphemous? _Why_ rewrite, reinterpret, and revolt the Gospels as Biblical Horror? _Can_ a horror novel be a Spiritual, Inspirational, and Transcendent religious experience? _Can_ horror be spiritually uplifting? _Can_ horror free you from sin? _Can_ horror inspire you to accept Jesus Christ as your Lord and Personal Saviour through suspense, mystery, terror, shock, and gore?

Yes!

Throughout His ministry, the eyes of the blind are opened, and the ears of the deaf are unstopped, and then the lame man leaps as an hart, and the tongue of the dumb sings. And He casts out demons from the unclean through horrific exorcism. Only in this unique tome are the exorcisms of Jesus Christ a truly Transcendent horror _and_ religious experience!

Is _The First Exorcist_ the perfect horror novel for you to read and keep you awake tonight?

- Are you a reader who dares read an absolutely unique novel: _both_ transcendent horror _and_ religious revelation?
- Are you a Christian who desires not only the inspiration of the Gospel, but truly experience the fear of God?
- Are you a horror aficionado who longs for exceptionally transcendent terror, horror, and revulsion?

ROBERT DWIGHT BROWN

The First Exorcist

FULL COLOR & ILLUSTRATED - RED LETTER EDITION
With the Words our Lord and Saviour in Red
& God the Father in Purple

Allonymous Books
A Division of Chi Xi Stigma Publishing Company, LLC

Dedicated to the Masters of Horror
From Edgar Allen Poe & H.P. Lovecraft
To William Peter Blatty & Stephen King & Neil Gaiman
Through your inspiration, I am freed to create
A Blood Gospel of Biblical Terror, Horror, and Revulsion!

Allonymous Books

A Division of Chi Xi Stigma Publishing Company, LLC

Trade Paperback— ISBN 13: 978-1-931608-60-2

Also Available: *The Harrowed Heart* — ISBN 13: 978-1-931608-48-0
Also Available: *The Machination of Vipers* — ISBN 13: 978-1-931608-71-8

Cover image: Bosch, Hieronymous, Follower of, *Christ In Limbo*, c, 1500-1599, Philadelphia Museum of Art, Philadelphia, Pennsylvania
Paper image:: http://www.myfreetextures.com/vintage-paper-texture-with-design/

Danse Macabre: To the modern reader, horror fiction began with Edgar Allen Poe continued to the weird supernatural fiction of H.P. Lovecraft and the horror of Richard Mattheson, Shirley Jackson, and Ray Bradbury, and concludes in the modern era with Stephen King. But *Danse Macabre* ("the Dance of Death") dates the horror genre to, at least, the Late Middle Ages through art, allegory, and music. But being scared by stories, no doubt, dates back to the primordial past with Cro-Magnon man sitting around the fire retelling the harrowing hunting of mammoths.

But _Why_ focus a retelling and re-imagining of the Gospel narrative as a horror novel? Shouldn't the Gospel narrative uplift, inspire, and demand devotion?

Is this why most of the masters of horror, have shied away from the Gospel narrative, or Christianity as a source of their horror? H.P. Lovecraft devoted himself to creating his own weird Cthulhu Mythos, most horror novels (and movies) are surprisingly agnostic. Sure, William Peter Blatty shocked readers and Hollywood audience members with *The Exorcist*, a novel (and subsequent movie) that brought an obscure Catholic rite into the mainstream light. I'm sure Protestants and non-religious alike are scared by the movie (and novel), but this a work designed to truly scare, terrify, and horrify Catholics.

The French film *Martyrs*, begins as a classic (if not horrifying) revenge movie, before morphing into testicle-clinching torture-porn. Yet, in the literal final moments of the motion picture, *Martyrs* reveals itself to be a truly transcendent religious experience. How could a movie of such shocking and revolting violence be transcendent? I love *Martyrs* as one of my all-time favorite films and I cannot answer this question, nor can I watch it _ever_ again. It is that disturbing.

And speaking of disturbing torture-porn: Mel Gibson's shocking and shockingly successful *The Passion of the Christ* took a passionate and myopic view of the suffering of Jesus Christ through His arrest, scourging, and crucifixion. As I sat in the theater awaiting the movie to begin, there were several groups of Christians each with their own minister preparing their congregations for the message of the movie: (which apparently is) that Jesus suffered and died for their sins. When the credits rolled and as the congregations of Christians wept for His suffering, I sat stunned by my enjoyment of such an exquisite horror movie. This is not a film in the tradition of Cecil B. DeMille, but Eli Roth. *The Passion* is classic 21st Century torture-porn.

When I decided that I wanted to finally write a horror novel in the vein of Stephen King, Clive Barker, or William Peter Blatty, what subject would I focus on? Slashers, demons, vampires, werewolves, ghosts, zombies? There are so many wonderful sub-genres to horror fiction, the possibilities seemed endless.

As I began preparing my mind for the grueling undertaking of writing a truly terrifying horror novel, I knew a few things. I wanted it to be based on a religious experience (not unlike *The Exorcist*), but one that hadn't been done to death (like *The Exorcist*). Then a disturbing thought occurred to me. One of the most horrifying scriptures I ever read as a young Catholic, one that haunted my dreams and caused many nights of nightmares was: *when Jesus asked a man with an unclean spirit, "What is thy name?" And he answered, saying, "My name is Legion: for we are many."* (Mk. 5:9). I knew because of this scripture and a certain other scripture (Mt. 27:52-53) that *The First Exorcist* and *The Harrowed Heart* (ISBN 13: 978-1-931608-48-0) would include two of the great tropes of horror fiction: exorcisms and zombies!

"Wait! What? There may be exorcisms in the Gospel narrative", you say, **"but there certainly aren't mother-f***ing zombies!"**

Of course there are!

Then *the graves were opened; and many bodies of the saints which slept arose, and after Jesus' resurrection, when they had come out of the tombs, they entered the holy city and appeared to many people* (Mt. 27:52-53)!

I had my answer! I could focus the Gospel narrative, and ratchet up the suspense, mystery, terror, shock, and gore but include exorcisms and mother-fucking zombies, amongst many other classic horror tropes, including a descent into Hell itself!

Why would you ever doubt me?

Author's Note:
The Gospels According to... Who?!?:
We all know, even the non-Christians amongst us, know that Matthew, Mark, Luke, and John wrote the Gospels. This is the singular Gospel Narrative that inspired the *The Greatest Story Ever Told,* the T.V. miniseries *Jesus of Nazareth,* the Broadway musical *Jesus Christ Superstar,* the controversial *The Last Temptation of Christ,* Mel Gibson's torture-porn *The Passion of the Christ,* and the epic(ally hilarious) *Monty Python's Life of Brian.*

But nowhere to be found amongst the great retellings of the Gospel Narrative do we find *The Gospel According to H.P. Lovecraft, The Gospel According to Neil Gaiman,* or *The Gospel According to Stephen King.*

H.P. Lovecraft created the *Necronomicon,* a fictional grimoire that thousands of Weird supernatural fans spent their teenaged years searching for. Imagine if he put his macabre mind to the Gospel Narrative (*minds blown!*). While Lovecraft was far more interested in gods older (far, far older) than Jesus the Christ, as a teenager I would have loved to have read a series of short stories of *The Christ Mythos.*

Neil Gaiman created the world of *The Sandman's* Dreaming populated by ancient creatures and gods, and with his *American Gods,* he doesn't (necessarily) neglect the Gospel Narrative, but instead focuses on the brutal, violent, and gory war between the old gods and the new gods (money, technology, media, celebrity and drugs). Neil has taken one element of theology that I truly, _truly_ believe in that the gods live and die by the number of their worshipers. Why else were the early followers of Jesus so adamant about obliterating the Greek, the Roman, the Norse, the Aztec, and the Gnostic religions (Note: I don't use the word "mythologies")?

And as for Stephen King, wouldn't you soil yourself to see him write a Blood Gospel of Biblical Horror?—What did you say?—Stephen King wrote *The Stand?* Ooh... so I guess he's been there and done that.

Since they haven't, can't (R.I.P. H.P.), or won't, then *I have* to.

Before I settled on *The First Exorcist* and *The Harrowing of the Inferno* (and *The Harrowed Heart*) as the title(s) of my (then unflippable) Blood Gospel of Biblical Horror, I was tempted (for the tiniest of moments) to call the novel *"The Gospel According to Stephen King"*. Blasphemy? Heresy? With my past works, I have used the term "allonymous" (meaning a work written in the name of a much more famous author) not only as a creative crutch, but as a font of great inspiration. As a Shakespearean nut, I was always struck by the fact that The Bard never wrote a Passion Play in his estimable *iambic-pentameter*, so I wrote *The Gospel According to Shakespeare: The Passion*[1]. I wondered what an erotic adaptation of *A Midsummer Night's Dream* would look like adapted by the Marquis de Sade, so I wrote *The Marquis de Sade's* A Midsummer Night's Wet Dream[2]. I wondered why the Holy Bible ends after the New Testament, so I wrote not only the Next Testament, but *The Holy Bible Trilogy*[3]. I wondered why Charles Dickens didn't write the story of Ebenezer's father (so clearly realized by a single line in *A Christmas Carol*), so I wrote *The Hauntings of Jeremiah & Ebenezer Scrooge*[4].

This allonymous writing is kind of my shtick.

But writing an allonymous novel "in the name" of a writer who is still alive, who is as famous as Stephen King is, and whose work isn't far, far, far into the public domain, my writer friends thought I would *court* legal action, so *The Gospel According to Stephen King* became *The First Exorcist* / *The Harrowing of the Inferno!*

So that's why I've been forced to write *The First Exorcist* / *The Harrowing of the Inferno* not as Stephen King would have written it (though I think I'm kind of close), not as H.P. Lovecraft would have written it (though he is in the public domain and probably doesn't have an estate to sue me), not as Matthew, Mark, Luke, and John would have written it (because they already wrote their Gospels two thousand years ago and this *isn't* it), but as **I would have written it** (there goes my allonymous shtick. *Shit!*)

---

1 *The Gospel According to Shakespeare: The Passion* (ISBN: 978-1-931608-30-5)
2 *Marquis de Sade's* A Midsummer Night's Wet Dream (ISBN: 978-1-931608-36-7)
3 *The Holy Bible Trilogy: The Old, New & Next Testaments* (ISBN: 978-1-931608-49-7)
4 *The Hauntings of Jeremiah & Ebenezer Scrooge* (ISBN: 978-1-931608-43-5)

Chapter 1
"She Who Is Without Sin"

HE **LORD GOD OF ISRAEL** SENT the angel Gabriel unto a hamlet of the Galilee, named Nazareth, to a virgin espoused to a man whose name was Joseph, of the house of David; and the virgin's name was Mary. And the angel came in unto her, and said, "Hail, thou that art highly favoured, the **LORD** is with thee: blessed art thou among women."

And when she saw him, his saying troubled her, and cast in her mind what manner of salutation this should be. And the angel said unto her, "Fear not, Mary: for thou hast found favour with **God**. And, Behold! thou shalt conceive in thy womb, and bring forth a **Son**, and shalt call **His** name **Jesus**. **He** shall be great, and shall be called the **Son** of the **Highest**: and the **LORD God** shall give unto **Him** the throne of **His** father David: and **He** shall reign over the house of Jacob for ever; and of

1

His kingdom there shall be no end."

Then said Mary unto the angel, "How shall this be, seeing I know not a man? "

And the angel answered and said unto her, "The Holy Ghost shall come upon thee, and the power of the Highest shall overshadow thee: therefore also that Holy Thing which shall be born of thee shall be called the Son of God. And, behold, thy cousin Elisabeth, she hath also conceived a son in her old age: and this is the sixth month with her, who was called barren. For with God nothing shall be impossible."

And Mary said, "Behold the handmaid of the LORD; be it unto me according to Thy word." And the angel departed from her.

There came a sound from Heaven as of a rushing mighty wind. Appeareth cloven tongues like as of fire! And Mary prayed:

O! Thy fiery tongue of the Psalm sung.
I yearn for Thy afire tongue. My passions wrung!
With child shalt I be? I, Eve's pure daughter.
Shalt my child be a Lamb led to slaughter?
When Rabbis observe my intact chaste fold
Shalt thy knowest still am I a virgin
 As the prophet Isaiah hath foretold.
  My lust come forth without original sin.
   Doth God take pride in my pure behaviour?
   My spirit hath rejoiced in God my Saviour.
    Why wast my own mother's menses unrotten?
    Immaculate Conception I begotten;
     Whense from the Creation as was designed!
     Thy tongue on my tongue. Our kisses entwined.
      O! stunned am I by Thy fiery tongue;

My lungs quick with breath. O! my flower stung
By Thy tongue's waspish sting. Thy tongue. 'M fraught!
Whenat God a child in my womb begot.
My bush burns with fire and yet not consumed
Is my hymen when my scion enwombed.
My distress to God cries in heresy.
Beneath me, LORD, the earth reels, rocks. Gramercy!
Up my nostrils smoke and devouring fire
From Thy mouth, glowing coals my sweat perspire.
O! my mountains smoke and tremble and quake.
Ride me like a cherub 'til my hips ache.
From the shame of voyeurs, darkness us covers
A canopy thick clouds divine lovers!
O! my climax flashes forth lightning
Routes my flower's orgasmic tightening.
Passion rains on me from the clouds hailstones.
His love eternal. Blessed am I alone!
No one comes from the Father except me!

When Joseph espoused to Mary, before they came together, he found his bethrothed with Child, though ignorant the Holy Ghost hath conceived of the Child. Then Joseph her husband, being a just man, and not willing to make her a public example, minded to put her away privily. But entered Satan into the mother of Joseph and she brought Mary to the scribes and Pharisees as a woman taken in adultery, and when they had set her in the midst.

The elders of Nazareth said unto Joseph, "Your bethrothed is taken in adultery, for she is found to be with child. Now Moses in the law commanded us, that such should be stoned: but what sayest thou?"

Howbeit Joseph held his tongue.

The Annunciation of Mary by an angel of the LORD!

Heretofore the mother of Joseph spoke with the forked tongue of the old serpent, called the Devil, and Satan, upon her lips for the devil can cite Scripture for his purpose. An evil soul producing holy witness is like a villain with a smiling cheek, a goodly apple rotten at the heart. And the mother of Joseph saith, "Ye elders of Nazareth speak in halves and considereth not the whole of the Law. Moses affords any man betrothed to a maid to take unto her his wife. My son hath giveth no occasions of speech against her, and he brings not up an evil name upon her, and saying nothing akin to 'I took this woman, and when I came to her, I found her not a maid!' The father of his harlot, and her mother, cannot take and bring forth the tokens of the harlot's virginity unto the elders of the city in the gate, how-beit, the elders of our city cannot take my son and chastise him, because the tokens of virginity be not found in the harlot for her hath no tokens of virginity! The virgin is with child?!? It is unnatural! It is blasphemous! Mary is a harlot! Mary is a whore! Ye all of Nazareth must bring out the whore to the door of her father's house, and the men of her city must stone her with stones that she die: because she hath wrought folly in Israel, to play the whore in her father's house: so shalt thou put evil away from among you!"

The men and the women and the children of Nazareth assembled themselves in a ring of fire and fury about Mary, with the **Holy Child** in her womb, and they stoned her with stones. Blood spat from a wound on her temple, the blood staining the tawny dirt scarlet. Mary fell to the ground, shielding she did the **Holy Child** in her womb. The stones rained like hail stones from a tempest of wrath, bruising her swelling breast, blackening her eyes until she wept blood, and crippling the hands

The mother of Joseph pridefully accuses Mary of adultery!

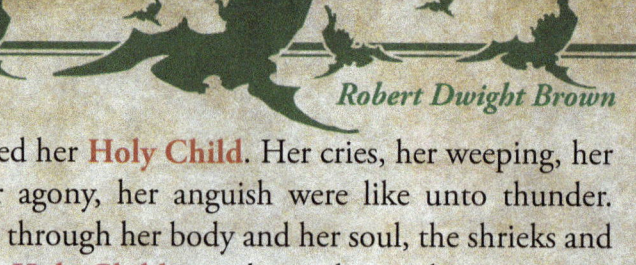

that protected her Holy Child. Her cries, her weeping, her wailing, her agony, her anguish were like unto thunder. Pain flashed through her body and her soul, the shrieks and howls of the Holy Child rent the earth asunder.

Lightning flashed in the heavens with the thunderous Anger of God and the tears of the angels rained down upon the village of Nazareth. But the torrent of torment staid not the hands of the Nazarenes, for Satan had entered into the Nazarenes all and still they stoned Mary with stones.

But while the Nazarenes stoned his betrothed with stones, behold, the angel of the LORD appeared unto him in the flesh, saying, "Joseph, thou son of David, fear not to take unto thee Mary thy wife: for that which is conceived in her is of the Holy Ghost. And she shall bring forth a Son, and thou shalt call His name Jesus: for He shall save His people from their sins."

Now all this was done, that it might be fulfilled which was spoken of the LORD by the prophet, saying, "Behold, a virgin shall be with child, and shall bring forth a son, and they shall call His name Emmanuel, which being interpreted is, 'God with us'."

Joseph fell upon the muck and covered Mary and the Holy Child in her womb with his own mortal remains, the stones of the stoning his skull cracked, his skin rent asunder, his blood bled, the bone of his skull fractured. The stones his ribs shattered, the splitters lacerated his lungs. The stones his jaw broken, his teeth loosed. The stones his vital remains bruised, the bleeding enclosed within his skin reeked like unto stench of death.

⸿ The angel of the LORD being clad in the whole armour of God, that he may be able to withstand in the evil day, and having done all, to stand. Stand therefore, having his loins girt about with truth, and having on the breastplate of righteousness; and his feet shod with the preparation of the gospel of peace; above all, taking the shield of faith, wherewith ye shall be able to quench all the fiery darts of the wicked. And take the helmet of salvation, and the sword of the **Spirit**, which is the word of **God**, he shielded the **Holy Child** and **His** mother.

And the angel of the **LORD** shielded within her womb the redemption through **His** blood, which beat as one with **His** mother's heart and her blood, without blemish from the stain of our mother Eve's original sin, from the moment of her own immaculate conception. Through her womb alone is born the forgiveness of sins, according to the riches of **His** grace; wherein **He** shalt abound toward us in all wisdom and prudence; **He** shalt make made known unto us the mystery of **His** will, according to **His** good pleasure which **He** hath purposed in **Himself**: that in the dispensation of the fulness of times **He** shall gather together in one all things in **Christ**, both which are in heaven, and which are on earth; even in **Him**: in whom also we shall obtain an inheritance, being predestinated according to the purpose of **Him** who worketh all things after the counsel of **His** own will: That we shall one day praise of **His** glory, all those who shall trust in **Christ**.

And upon seeing the angel of the **LORD** shielding Mary believed to be carrying a child conceived of sin, the Nazarenes then saw the **Spirit** of **God** descending like a dove, and lighting upon Mary, carrying a **Child** who would bare our sins in **His** own body on the tree, that we, being dead to sins, should live unto righteousness by **Whose** stripes ye were healed. And lo a voice from heaven, saying, "**Within her womb is My beloved Son, in whom I AM well pleased.**" And they cast aside their stones to fall upon the earth, and Satan abandoned all of them whom he had entered, returning them to their lives, their homes, and their faith in the LORD.

The Holy Child reached out His forming hand and touched the womb of His mother, Mary, and the Holy Ghost radiated a warmth that healed her of her wounds; her bones broken mended; her teeth loosed fit snug in their sockets, her vital remains no longer were bruised and bleeding.

The radiant warmth of the Holy Ghost entered into Mary's betrothed, Joseph of Nazareth of Galilee, and healed him of his wounds; his bones broken mended, his teeth loosed fit snug in their sockets, his vital remains no longer were bruised and bleeding. ✝

Chapter 2
"Massacre of Innocents"

OW WHEN **HE** WAS BORN IN Bethlehem of Judaea in the days of Herod the king, behold, there came wise men from the east to Jerusalem, saying, "Where is **He** that is born **King of the Jews**? for we have seen **His** star in the east, and are come to worship **Him**."

When Herod the king had heard these things, he was troubled, and all Jerusalem with him. And when he had gathered all the elders, and the chief priests and scribes of the people together in the house of his father-in-law, the High-Priest Simon son of Boethus, he demanded of them where the **Messiah** should be born.

And there was great murmuring and consternation because they knew well the prophecy of Daniel that the seventy weeks were determined upon their people and upon their holy city, to finish the transgression, and to make an end of sins, and to make reconciliation for iniquity, and to bring in everlasting righteousness, and to seal up the vision and prophecy, and to anoint the most Holy. The scribes had figured the seventy weeks of years and knoweth three periods of forty-nine years, four-hundred-and-thirty-four years and a final week of seven years and all beginning when it had come to pass.

And given the figures and the calculations, they all knew their generation shall not pass, till all of the prophecy of the seventy weeks be fulfilled when after threescore and two weeks shall the Messiah be cut off. And if the Messiah's hands and feet are to be pierced according to the words of Zechariah the prophet and it was written also that "His body shall not remain all night upon the tree, but thou shalt in any wise bury Him that day; (for he that is hanged is accursed of God;) that thy land be not defiled, which the LORD thy God giveth thee for an inheritance." The scribes of Herod's Sanhedrin knew of their knowledge that the Messiah would be crucified by the procurator of Rome.

And furthermore, did not Herod the king rebuild Solomon's temple, even in troublous times under the banner of Rome, in fulfilment of the prophecy? In all of the history of the world, from the creation of Adam until coming of the Messiah and the new heaven and the new earth, the scribes knew the birth of the Messiah was at hand and they were filled with the dread that their power over land Israel was at an end.

And watchful of the descendants of David the king were they for they knew the words the LORD saith unto David: "When thy days be fulfilled, and thou shalt sleep with thy fathers, I will set up thy seed after thee, which shall proceed out of thy bowels, and I will establish His kingdom. He shall build an house for My name, and I will stablish the throne of His kingdom for ever. I will be His Father, and He shall be My Son. If He commit iniquity, I will chasten Him with the rod of men, and with the stripes of the children of men: But My mercy shall not depart away from Him, as I took it from Saul, whom I put away before thee. And thine house and thy kingdom shall be established for ever before thee: thy throne shall be established for ever."

For these were the sons of David, which were born unto him in Hebron; the firstborn Amnon, of Ahinoam the Jezreelitess; the second Daniel, of Abigail the Carmelitess: The third, Absalom the son of Maachah the daughter of Talmai king of Geshur: the fourth, Adonijah the son of Haggith: The fifth, Shephatiah of Abital: the sixth, Ithream by Eglah his wife. These six were born unto him in Hebron; and there he reigned seven years and six months: and in Jerusalem he reigned thirty and three years. And these were born unto him in Jerusalem; Shimea, and Shobab, and Nathan, and Solomon, four, of Bathshua the daughter of Ammiel: Ibhar also, and Elishama, and Eliphelet, And Nogah, and Nepheg, and Japhia, And Elishama, and Eliada, and Eliphelet, nine. These were all the sons of David, beside the sons of the concubines, and Tamar their sister. And Solomon's son was Rehoboam, Abia his son, Asa his son, Jehoshaphat his son, Joram his son, Ahaziah his son, Joash his son, Amaziah his son, Azariah his son, Jotham his son. Ahaz his son, Hezekiah his son, Manasseh his son, Amon his son, Josiah his son. And the sons of Josiah were, the firstborn Johanan, the second Jehoiakim, the third Zedekiah, the fourth Shallum. And the sons of Jehoiakim: Jeconiah his son, Zedekiah his son. And the sons of Jeconiah; Assir, Salathiel his son,

Malchiram also, and Pedaiah, and Shenazar, Jecamiah, Hoshama, and Nedabiah. And the sons of Pedaiah were, Zerubbabel, and Shimei: and the sons of Zerubbabel; Meshullam, and Hananiah, and Shelomith their sister: And Hashubah, and Ohel, and Berechiah, and Hasadiah, Jushabhesed, five. And the sons of Hananiah; Pelatiah, and Jesaiah: the sons of Rephaiah, the sons of Arnan, the sons of Obadiah, the sons of Shechaniah. And the sons of Shechaniah; Shemaiah: and the sons of Shemaiah; Hattush, and Igeal, and Bariah, and Neariah, and Shaphat, six. And the sons of Neariah; Elioenai, and Hezekiah, and Azrikam, three. And the sons of Elioenai were, Hodaiah, and Eliashib, and Pelaiah, and Akkub, and Johanan, and Dalaiah, and Anani, seven.

"Where shall the **Messiah** be born," Herod demanded of their murmurings and consternations. And they said unto him, "In Bethlehem of Judaea: for thus it is written by the prophet, 'But thou, Bethlehem Ephratah, though thou be little among the thousands of Judah, yet out of thee shall **He** come forth unto me that is to be ruler in Israel; whose goings forth have been from of old, from everlasting. Therefore will **He** give them up, until the time that she which travaileth hath brought forth: then the remnant of his brethren shall return unto the children of Israel. And **He** shall stand and feed in the strength of the **LORD**, in the majesty of the name of the **LORD His God**; and they shall abide: for now shall he be great unto the ends of the earth. And this man shall be the peace, when the Assyrian shall come into our land: and when he shall tread in our palaces, then shall we raise against **Him** seven shepherds, and eight principal men.' "

Then Herod, when he had privily called these pagan astronomers, these purported wise men, enquired of them diligently what time the star appeared, so that he could learn the knowledge of the age of the children of Bethlehem he would massacre. Herod was not willing in indiscriminately murder the first born sons of Bethlehem as the **LORD God of Israel** did at midnight on that night so long ago in Egypt when the **LORD** smote all the firstborn in the land of Egypt, from the firstborn of Pharaoh that sat on his throne unto the firstborn of the captive that was in the dungeon; and all the firstborn of cattle. And Pharaoh rose up in the night, he, and all his servants, and all the Egyptians; and there was a great cry in Egypt; for there was not a house where there was not one dead. Herod, knowing the knowledge he would skulk in the shadows so that the future scriptures of would-be scribes would not paint Herod the king in a murderous light.

And Herod sent them to Bethlehem, and said, "Go and search diligently for the **Holy Child**; and when ye have found **Him**, bring me word again, that I may come and worship **Him** also."

When they had heard the king, they departed; and, lo! the star, which they saw in the east, went before them, till it came and stood over where the **Holy Child** lain in the manger. When they saw the star, they rejoiced with exceeding great joy. And when they were come into the house, they saw the **Holy Child** with Mary **His** mother, and fell down, and worshipped **Him**: and when they had opened their treasures, they presented unto **Him** gifts; gold, and frankincense and myrrh.

And being warned of **LORD God of Israel**, this strange singular **God** of a strange singular people, in a dream that they should not return to Herod, they departed into their own country another way.

Then Herod the king, when he saw that the pagan astrologers, those wise men, mocked him, in-

sulted him, emasculated him, his wrath exceeded, and knew of the world of the **LORD** that: happy shall he be, that taketh and dasheth thy little ones against the stones. Knoweth Herod not that his own **LORD God of Israel** commanded the Israelites to utterly destroy all that was in the city of Jericho, both man and woman, young and old, and ox, and sheep, and ass, with the edge of the sword. Herod was a kind king who commanded and sent forth is soldiers with reserved orders to slay all the children that were in Bethlehem, and in all the coasts thereof, from two years old and under, according to the time which he had diligently inquired of the wise men.

For it was the Passover, when three times in a year shall all Israel's males appear before the **LORD thy God** in the place which **He** hath chosen, Jerusalem; in the feast of unleavened bread, and in the feast of weeks, and in the feast of tabernacles: and they shall not appear before the **LORD** empty. And there was no room for the holy family in the inn because of the feast of the unleavened bread. The lands of Judaea and the coasts therein were filled to overflowing with families, both man and woman, young and old, and ox, and sheep, and ass.

And the soldiers entered into each abode and into every inn and manger and slew the children under the age of two with their swords, and the mothers of the children were exceedingly grieved and their weeping and their wailing pierced the night as a foul wind. The women gnashed their teeth and clawed at the eyes of the soldiers as good women should, but their plight was for naught. The necks of their children were cut to the bone and their blood bundled them in the comforting swaddling clothes of death. And the sounds of the breaking of

The massacre of the innocents and innocence of Bethlehem by King Herod!

their backs and the snapping of their necks echoed throughout the streets a trumpet sounding the coming of a pale horse: and his name that sat on him was Death, and Hell followed with him. The soldiers discarded their children into the street like they were nothing more than the waste of urine and excrement from chamber pots and trampled under the boots of the soldiers. And others of their children were thrown onto fires, their screams were a smoke that blotted out the moon on the cloudless night. The weeping and the wailing the women joined in the chorus of the paleful song of death.

Then was fulfilled that which was spoken by Jeremiah the prophet, saying, "A voice was heard in Ramah, lamentation, and bitter weeping; Rachel weeping for her children refused to be comforted for her children, because they were not."

And when they were departed, behold, the angel of the LORD appeareth to Joseph in a dream, saying, "Arise, and take the young Child and His mother, and flee into Egypt, and be thou there until I bring thee word: for Herod will seek the young Child to destroy Him."

When he arose, he took the young Child and His mother by night, and departed into Egypt: And lived there until the death of Herod: that it might be fulfilled which the LORD by the prophet spoke, saying, "When Israel was a child, then I loved Him, and called My Son out of Egypt."

But when Herod died, behold, an angel of the LORD appeareth in a dream to Joseph in Egypt, saying, "Arise, and take the Holy Child and His mother, and go into the land of Israel: for they are dead which sought the Holy Child's life." And he arose, and took the Holy Child and His mother, and came into the land of Israel.

But when he heard that Archelaus did reign in Judaea in the room of his father Herod, he was afraid to go thither: notwithstanding, being warned of **God** in a dream, he turned aside into the parts of Galilee: And he came and dwelt in a city called Nazareth: that it might be fulfilled which was spoken by the prophets, "**He** shall be called a Nazarene."

Chapter 3
"Regaineth Paradise"

OW HAD THE GREAT PRO-
claimer, with a voice more awful than the
sound of trumpet, cried repentance, and
Heaven's kingdom nigh at hand to all bap-
tized. To **His** great baptism flocked with awe the regions
round, and with them came from Nazareth the son of Joseph deemed to the flood Jordan, came as then obscure,
unmarked, unknown. But John the Baptist soon descried,
divinely warned, and witness bore as to his worthier, and
would have resigned to **Him** his heavenly office. Nor was
long his witness unconfirmed: on him baptized heaven
opened, and in likeness of a Dove the **Spirit** descended,
while the **Father**'s voice from Heaven pronounced **Him**
His beloved **Son**.

That Satan heard, who, roving still about the

21

Milton, John *Paradise Regained* abridged, adapted from, and expanded world, at that assembly famed would not be last, and, with the voice divine nigh thunder-struck, the exalted man to whom such high attest was given a while surveyed with wonder; then, with envy fraught and rage, flies to his place, nor rests, but in mid air to council summons all his mighty peers, within thick clouds and dark tenfold involved, a gloomy consistory; and them amidst, with looks aghast and sad, he thus bespake: "O! ancient Powers of Air and this wide world (for much more willingly I mention Air, this our old conquest, than remember Hell, our hated habitation), well ye know how many ages, as the years of men, this universe we have possessed, and ruled in manner at our will the affairs of Earth, since Adam and his facile consort Eve lost Paradise, deceived by me, though since with dread attending when that fatal wound shall be inflicted by the seed of Eve upon my head.

"I saw the Prophet do him reverence; on him, rising out of the water, heaven above the clouds unfold her crystal doors; thence on his head a perfect Dove descend (whate'er it meant); and out of heaven the sovereign voice I heard, 'This is my Son beloved,– in Him am pleased.' His mother, than, is mortal, but His Sire he who obtains the monarchy of Heaven; and what will He not do to advance His Son?

"Ye see our danger on the utmost edge of hazard, which admits no long debate, but must with something sudden be opposed (not force, but well-couched fraud, well-woven snares), ere in the head of nations he appear, their king, their leader, and supreme on Earth."

The devil's infernal crew, distracted and surprised with deep dismay at these sad tidings. But no time was then for long indulgence to their fears or grief: unanimous they all commit the care and management of this man enterprise to him, their great Dictator, whose attempt at first against mankind so well had thrived in Adam's overthrow.

The LORD, and all heaven admiring stood a space; then into hymns burst forth, and in celestial measures moved, circling the throne and singing, while the hand sung with the voice, and this the argument: "Victory and triumph to the Son of God, now entering his great duel, not of arms, but to vanquish by wisdom hellish wiles! The Father knows the Son; therefore secure ventures His filial virtue, though untried, against whatever may tempt, whatever seduce, allure, or terrify, or undermine. Be frustrate, all ye stratagems of Hell, and, devilish machinations, come to nought!"

So they in heaven their odes and vigils tuned. Meanwhile the Son of God, who yet some days lodged in Bethabara, where John baptized, musing and much revolving in his breast how best the mighty work he might begin of Saviour to mankind, and which way first publish His Godlike office now mature, one day forth walked alone, the Spirit leading and His deep thoughts, the better to converse with solitude, till, far from track of men, thought following thought, and step by step led on, he entered now the bordering Desert wild, and, with dark shades and rocks environed round, his holy meditations thus pursued.

An aged man walketh in the Desert wild, when an angel of the LORD appeared unto him in a flame of fire out of the midst of a bush: and he looked, and, behold, the bush burned with fire, and the bush was not consumed, and the LORD called unto him out of the midst of the bush and said "Whence comest thou?" Then the aged man answered the LORD, and said, "As the God of this world I hath blinded the minds of them which believe not, lest the light of the glorious gospel of

Christ, who is the image of God, should shine unto them!"

And the LORD saith unto the aged man, "Hast thou considered My Son, I hath made Him to be sin for man, Who knew no sin; that they might be made the righteousness of God in Him. And I know that He is manifest to take away the sins of the world; and in Him is no sin.

"Forasmuch as they know that they are not redeemed with corruptible things, as silver and gold, from their vain conversation received by tradition from their fathers; but with the precious blood of Christ, as of a lamb without blemish and without spot: Who verily was foreordained before the foundation of the world, but was manifest in these last times for them, who by Him do believe in God, that shalt raiseth Him up from the dead, and gave Him glory; that your faith and hope might be in God.

And the aged man answered the LORD, and saith, "Doth Jesus the Nazarene fear God for nought? Hast not Thou made an hedge about Him, and about His house, and about all that He hath on every side? Thou hast blessed the work of His hands. But letteth me put forth mine hand now, and showeth unto Him all the kingdoms of the world and tempteth with worldly rewards if He shalt worship me, and all shall be His, and He shalt worship me!"

And the LORD said unto the aged man, "Behold, all that He hath is in thy power; only upon Himself put not forth thine hand to tempt My beloved Son; in Him I AM well pleased. But let no man say when he is tempted, 'I am tempted of God': for God cannot be tempted with evil, neither tempteth he any man: but every man is tempted, when he is drawn away of his own lust, and enticed. Then when lust hath conceived, it bringeth forth sin: and sin, when it is finished, bringeth forth

---

The Devil as an aged man tempts Him in the desert of the wilderness!

death. Every good gift and every perfect gift is from above, and cometh down from the Father of lights, with whom is no variableness, neither shadow of turning. Of His own will begat He us with the word of truth, that they should be a kind of firstfruits of my beloved Son; in whom I AM well pleased."

Full forty days He passed– whether on hill sometimes, anon in shady vale, each night under the covert of some ancient oak or cedar to defend Him from the dew, or harboured in one cave, is not revealed; nor tasted human food, nor hunger felt, till those days ended; hungered then at last among wild beasts. They at His sight grew mild, nor sleeping Him nor waking harmed; His walk the fiery serpent fled and noxious worm; the lion and fierce tiger glared aloof.

But now an aged man in rural weeds, following, as seemed, the quest of some stray eye, or withered sticks to gather, which might serve against a winter's day, when winds blow keen, to warm Him wet returned from field at eve, He saw approach; who first with curious eye perused Him, then with words thus uttered spake:–

"Sir," said the aged man, "what ill chance hath brought Thee to this place, so far from path or road of men, who pass in troop or caravan? For single none durst ever, who returned, and dropt not here his carcass, pined with hunger and with drougth. I ask the rather, and the more admire, for that to me Thou seem'st the man whom late our new baptizing Prophet at the ford of Jordan honoured so, and called thee Son of God."

To whom the Son of God saith, "Who brought Me hither will bring Me hence; no other guide I seek."

"By miracle he may," replied the swain; "What other way I see not; for we here live on tough roots and stubs, to thirst inured more than the camel, and to drink go far– men to much misery and hardship born. But, if **Thou** be the **Son of God**, command that out of these hard stones be made **Thee** bread; so shalt **Thou** save **Thyself**, and us relieve with food, whereof we wretched seldom taste."

He ended, and the **Son of God** replied, **"Think'st thou such force in bread? Is it not written (for I discern thee other than thou seem'st), man lives not by bread only, but each word proceeding from the mouth of God, Who fed our fathers here with manna? In the Mount Moses was forty days, nor eat nor drank; and forty days Elijah without food wandered this barren waste; the same I now. Why dost thou, then, suggest to Me distrust knowing who I AM, as I know who thou art?"**

Whom thus answered the Arch-Fiend, now undisguised saith, "'Tis true, I am that Spirit unfortunate who, leagued with millions more in rash revolt, kept not my happy station, but was driven with them from bliss to the bottomless Deep– yet to that hideous place not so confined by rigour unconniving but that oft, leaving my dolorous prison, I enjoy large liberty to round this globe of Earth, or range in the Air; nor from the Heaven of heavens hath he excluded my resort sometimes.

"I came, among the Sons of **God**, when he gave up into my hands Uzzean Job, to prove him, and illustrate his high worth; and, when to all his Angels he proposed to draw the proud king Ahab into fraud. Though I have lost much lustre of my native brightness, lost to be beloved of **God**, I have not lost to love, at least contemplate and admire, what I see excellent in good, or fair, or virtuous.

"What can be then less in me than desire to see

thee and approach thee, whom I know declared the **Son of God**, to hear attent **Thy** wisdom, and behold **Thy God**like deeds? Men generally think me much a foe to all mankind. By them I lost not what I lost; rather by them I gained what I have gained, and with them dwell copartner in these regions of the World, if not disposer– lend them oft my aid, oft my advice by presages and signs, and answers, oracles, portents, and dreams, whereby they may direct their future life. Envy, they say, excites me, thus to gain companions of my misery and woe! This wounds me most (what can it less?) that Man, man fallen, shall be restored, I never more."

To whom **He** sternly thus replied, "**Deservedly thou griev'st, composed of lies from the beginning, and in lies wilt end, who boast'st release from Hell, and leave to come into the Heaven of heavens. The happy place imparts to thee no happiness, no joy– rather inflames thy torment, representing lost bliss, to thee no more communicable; so never more in Hell than when in Heaven. What but thy malice moved thee to misdeem of righteous Job, then cruelly to afflict him with all inflictions? But his patience won.**

"**But this thy glory shall be soon retrenched; no more shalt thou by oracling abuse the Gentiles; henceforth oracles are ceased, and thou no more with pomp and sacrifice shalt be enquired at Delphos or elsewhere– at least in vain, for they shall find thee mute. God hath now sent His living Oracle into the world to teach His final will, and sends His Spirit of Truth henceforth to dwell in pious hearts, an inward oracle to all truth requisite for men to know.**"

So spake our **Saviour**; but the subtle Fiend, though inly stung with anger and disdain, dissembled, and this answer smooth returned, "If it may stand him more in stead to lie, say and unsay, feign, flatter, or abjure? Hard are the ways of truth, and rough to walk, smooth on the tongue discoursed, pleasing to the ear, and tunable as sylvan pipe or song; what wonder, then, if I delight to hear her dictates from **Thy** mouth?"

To whom **He**, with unaltered brow saith, **"Thy coming hither, though I know thy scope, I bid not, or forbid. Do as thou find'st permission from above; thou canst not more."**

He added not; and Satan, bowling low his gray dissimulation, disappeared, into thin air diffused: for now began night with her sullen wing to double-shade the desert; fowls in their clay nests were couched; and now wild beasts came forth the woods to roam.

For Satan, with sly preface to return, had left **Him** vacant, and with speed was gone up to the middle region of thick air, where all his Potentates in council sate.

It was the hour of night, when thus the **Son** communed in silent walk, then laid **Him** down under the hospitable covert nigh of trees thick interwoven. There **He** slept, and dreamed, as appetite is wont to dream, of meats and drinks, nature's refreshment sweet. **Him** thought **He** by the brook of Cherith stood, and saw the ravens with their horny beaks food to Elijah bringing even and morn– though ravenous, taught to abstain from what they brought. Thus wore out night; and now the harald Lark left his ground-nest, high towering to descry the Morn's approach, and greet her with his song.

Up to a hill anon **His** steps **He** reared, from

whose high top to ken the prospect round, if cottage were
in view, sheep-cote, or herd; but cottage, herd, or sheep-
cote, none he saw– only in a bottom saw a pleasant grove,
with chaunt of tuneful birds resounding loud. **He** viewed it
round; when suddenly a man before **Him** stood, not rustic
as before, but seemlier clad, as one in city or court or palace
bred, and with fair speech these words to **Him** addressed
saying, "With granted leave officious I return, but much
more wonder that the **Son of God** in this wild solitude so
long should bide, of all things destitute, and, well I know,
not without hunger.

"Others of some note, as story tells, have trod this wilderness: the fugitive Bond-woman, with her son, outcast
Nebaioth, yet found here relief by a providing Angel; all the
race of Israel here had famished, had not **God** rained from
heaven manna; and that Prophet bold, native of Thebez,
wandering here, was fed twice by a voice inviting him to eat.
Of **Thee** those forty days none hath regard, forty and more
deserted here indeed."

To whom thus **He** saith, "**What conclud'st thou
hence? They all had need; I, as thou seest, have none.**"

Our **Saviour**, lifting up **His** eyes, beheld, in ample
space under the broadest shade, a table richly spread in regal mode, with dishes piled and meats of noblest sort and
savour– beasts of chase, or fowl of game, in pastry built, or
from the spit, or boiled, grisamber-steamed; all fish, from
sea or shore, freshet or purling brook, of shell or fin, and
exquisitest name, for which was drained pontus, and Lu-
crine bay, and Afric coast. Alas! how simple, to these cates
compared, was that crude apple that diverted Eve! And
at a stately sideboard, by the wine, that fragrant
smell diffused, in order stood tall stripling youths
rich-clad, of fairer hue than Ganymed or Hylas; dis-

tant more, under the trees now tripped, now solemn stood, nymphs of Diana's train, and Naiades with fruits and flowers from Amalthea's horn, and ladies of the Hesperides, that seemed fairer than feigned of old, or fabled since of faery damsels met in forest wide by knights of Logres, or of Lyones, lancelot, or Pelleas, or Pellenore. And all the while harmonious airs were heard of chiming strings or charming pipes; and winds of gentlest gale Arabian odours fanned from their soft wings, and Flora's earliest smells.

Such was the splendour; and the Tempter now his invitation earnestly renewed, saying, "What doubts the **Son of God** to sit and eat? These are not fruits forbidden; no interdict defends the touching of these viands pure; their taste no knowledge works, at least of evil, but life preserves, destroys life's enemy, hunger, with sweet restorative delight. What doubt'st thou, **Son of God**? Sit down and eat."

To whom thus **He** temperately saith, **"Said'st thou not that to all things I had right? And who withholds My power that right to use? Shall I receive by gift what of My own, when and where likes Me best, I can command? I can at will, doubt not, as soon as thou, command a table in this wilderness, and call swift flights of Angels ministrant, arrayed in glory, on My cup to attend: why shouldst thou, then, obtrude this diligence in vain, where no acceptance it can find? And with My hunger what hast thou to do? Thy pompous delicacies I contemn, and count thy specious gifts no gifts, but guiles."**

To whom thus answered Satan, male-content:— "But I see what I can do or offer is suspect. Of these things others quickly will dispose, whose pains have earned the far-fet spoil." With that both table and provision vanished quite, with sound of harpies' wings and talons heard. ""By hunger, that each other creature tames, **Thou** art not to be harmed, therefore not moved; **Thy** temperance, invincible besides, for no allurement yields to appetite; and all **Thy** heart is set on high designs, high actions.

"**Thou** art unknown, unfriended, low of birth, a carpenter **Thy Father** known, **Thyself** bred up in poverty and straits at home, lost in a desert here and hunger-bit. Which way, or from what hope, dost **Thou** aspire to greatness? herefore, if at great things thou wouldst arrive, get riches first, get wealth, and treasure heap— not difficult, if **Thou** hearken to me. Riches are mine, fortune is in my hand; they whom I favour thrive in wealth amain, while virtue, valour, wisdom, sit in want."

To whom thus **He** patiently replied:— **"Yet wealth without these three is impotent to gain dominion, or to keep it gained— witness those ancient empires of the earth, in highth of all their flowing wealth dissolved; but men endued with these have oft attained, in lowest poverty, to highest deeds— Gideon, and Jephtha, and the shepherd lad whose offspring on the throne of Juda sate so many ages, and shall yet regain that seat, and reign in Israel without end. Among the heathen (for throughout the world to Me is not unknown what hath been done worthy of memorial) canst thou not remember Quintius, Fabricius, Curius, Regulus? For I esteem those names of men so poor, who could do mighty things, and could contemn riches, though offered from the hand of kings. And what in Me seems wanting but that I may also in this poverty as soon accomplish what they did, perhaps and more? Extol not riches, then, the toil of fools, the wise man's cumbrance, if not snare; more apt to slacken virtue and abate her edge than prompt her to do aught may merit praise.**

What if with like aversion I reject riches and realms! Yet not for that a crown, golden in shew, is but a wreath of thorns, brings dangers, troubles, cares, and sleepless nights, to him who wears the regal diadem, when on his shoulders each man's burden lies; for therein stands the office of a king, his honour, virtue, merit, and chief praise, that for the public all this weight he bears.

"Yet he who reigns within himself, and rules passions, desires, and fears, is more a king– which every wise and virtuous man attains; and who attains not, ill aspires to rule cities of men, or headstrong multitudes, subject himself to anarchy within, or lawless passions in him, which he serves. But to guide nations in the way of truth by saving doctrine, and from error lead to know, and, knowing, worship God aright, is yet more kingly. This attracts the soul, governs the inner man, the nobler part; that other o'er the body only reigns, and oft by force– which to a generous mind so reigning can be no sincere delight. Besides, to give a kingdom hath been thought greater and nobler done, and to lay down far more magnanimous, than to assume. Riches are needless, then, both for themselves, and for thy reason why they should be sought– to gain a sceptre, oftest better missed."

Satan stood a while as mute, confounded what to say, what to reply, confuted and convinced of his weak arguing and fallacious drift; at length, collecting all his serpent wiles, with soothing words renewed, him thus accosts, saying:

"Then hear, O! Son of David, virgin-born! For

Son of God to me is yet in doubt. Of the Messiah I have
heard foretold by all the Prophets; of Thy birth, at length
announced by Gabriel, with the first I knew, and of the angelic song in Bethlehem field, on Thy birth-night, that sung
thee Saviour born. From that time seldom have I ceased
to eye Thy infancy, Thy childhood, and Thy youth, Thy
manhood last, though yet in private bred; till, at the ford of
Jordan, whither all flocked to the Baptist, I among the rest
(though not to be baptized), by voice from heaven heard
Thee pronounced the Son of God beloved.

"Thenceforth I thought Thee worth my nearer view
and narrower scrutiny, that I might learn in what degree or
meaning Thou art called the Son of God, which bears no
single sense. The Son of God I also am, or was; and, if I was,
I am; relation stands: all men are Sons of God; yet Thee I
thought in some respect far higher so declared.

"Therefore I watched Thy footsteps from that hour,
and followed thee still on to this waste wild, where, by all
best conjectures, I collect Thou art to be my fatal enemy.
Good reason, then, if I beforehand seek to understand my
adversary, who and what He is; His wisdom, power, intent;
by parle or composition, truce or league, to win Him, or
win from Him what I can.

"And opportunity I here have had to try Thee, sift
Thee, and confess have found thee proof against all temptation, as a rock of adamant and as a centre, firm to the
utmost of mere man both wise and good, not more; for
honours, riches, kingdoms, glory, have been before con-
temned, and may again. Therefore, to know what more
Thou art than man, worth naming the Son of God by
voice from Heaven, another method I must now
begin."

The Devil takes Him to the pinnacle of the Temple!

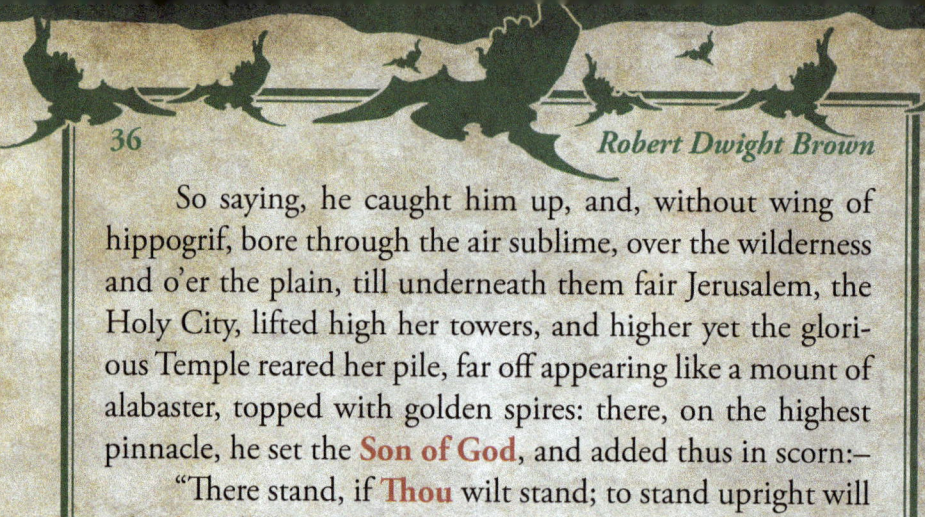

So saying, he caught him up, and, without wing of hippogrif, bore through the air sublime, over the wilderness and o'er the plain, till underneath them fair Jerusalem, the Holy City, lifted high her towers, and higher yet the glorious Temple reared her pile, far off appearing like a mount of alabaster, topped with golden spires: there, on the highest pinnacle, he set the **Son of God**, and added thus in scorn:—

"There stand, if **Thou** wilt stand; to stand upright will ask **Thee** skill. I to **Thy Father**'s house have brought **Thee**, and highest placed: highest is best. Now shew **Thy** progeny; if not to stand, cast **Thyself** down. Safely, if **Son of God**; for it is said of the **Lord**, 'He is **Thy** refuge and **Thy** fortress: **Thy God**; in him will **Thee** trust. Surely he shall deliver **Thee** from the snare of the fowler, and from the noisome pestilence. He shall cover **Thee** with his feathers, and under his wings shalt **Thou** trust: his truth shall be **Thy** shield and buckler. **Thou** shalt not be afraid for the terror by night; nor for the arrow that flieth by day; nor for the pestilence that walketh in darkness; nor for the destruction that wasteth at noonday. A thousand shall fall at **Thy** side, and ten thousand at **Thy** right hand; but it shall not come nigh **Thee**. Only with **Thine** eyes shalt thou behold and see the reward of the wicked. Because **Thou** hast made the **LORD**, which is **Thy** refuge, even the most **High**, **Thy** habitation; there shall no evil befall **Thee**, neither shall any plague come nigh **Thy** dwelling. For **He** shall give **His** angels charge over **Thee**, to keep **Thee** in all **Thy** ways. They shall bear **Thee** up in their hands, lest thou dash **Thy** foot against a stone. **Thou** shalt tread upon the lion and adder: the young lion and the dragon shalt **Thou** trample under feet."

"Also it is written, 'Tempt not the Lord thy God.'"

Perplexed and troubled at his bad success the Tempter stood, nor had what to reply, discovered in his fraud, thrown from his hope so oft, and the persuasive rhetoric that sleeked his tongue, and won so much on Eve, so little here, nay lost. But Eve was Eve; this far his over-match, who, self-deceived and rash, beforehand had no better weighed the strength he was to cope with, or his own. But— as a man who had been matchless held in cunning, over-reached where least he thought, to salve his credit, and for very spite, still will be tempting him who foils him still, and never cease, though to his shame the more; or as a swarm of flies in vintage-time, about the wine-press where sweet must is poured, beat off, returns as oft with humming sound; or surging waves against a solid rock, though all to shivers dashed, the assault renew,

"Think not so slight of glory, therein least resembling Thy great Father. He seeks glory, and for His glory all things made, all things orders and governs; nor content in Heaven, by all His Angels glorified, requires glory from men, from all men, good or bad, wise or unwise, no difference, no exemption. Above all sacrifice, or hallowed gift, glory He requires, and glory his receives, promiscuous from all nations, Jew, or Greek, or Barbarous, nor exception hath declared; from us, his foes pronounced, glory his exacts."

"All things are best fulfilled in their due time; and time there is for all things, Truth hath said. If of My reign Prophetic Writ hath told that it shall never end, so, when begin the Father in his purpose hath decreed— He in Whose hand all times and seasons rowl. What if He hath decreed that I shall first be tried in humble state, and things adverse, by tribulations, injuries, insults, contempts, and scorns, and snares, and violence, suffering, abstaining, quietly expecting without distrust or doubt, that He may know what I can suffer, how obey? Who best can suffer best can do, best reign who first well hath obeyed– just trial ere I merit My exaltation without change or end. But what concerns it thee when I begin My everlasting Kingdom? Why art thou solicitous? What moves thy inquisition? Know'st thou not that My rising is thy fall, and My promotion will be thy destruction?"

"All hope is lost of my reception into grace; what worse? For where no hope is left is left no fear. I would be at the worst; worst is my port, my harbour, and my ultimate repose, the end I would attain, my final good. My error was my error, and my crime my crime; whatever, for itself condemned, and will alike be punished, whether thou reign or reign not– though to that gentle brow willingly I could fly, and hope thy reign, from that placid aspect and meek regard, rather than aggravate my evil state, would stand between me and Thy Father's ire (Whose ire I dread more than the fire of Hell) a shelter and a kind of shading cool interposition, as a summer's cloud. If I, then, to the worst that can be haste, why move Thy feet so slow to what is best? No wonder; for, though in thee be united what of perfection can in man be found, or human nature can receive, consider Thy life hath yet been private, most part spent at home, scarce viewed the Galilean towns, and once a year Jerusalem, few days' short sojourn; and what thence couldst thou observe?"

With that (such power was given him then), he took the Son of God up unto the City of the

The Devil takes Him to the seven hills of Rome!

Seven Hills shewed unto **Him** the ruler of all the kingdoms of the world in a moment of time: "The city which thou seest no other deem than great and glorious Rome, Queen of the Earth so far renowned, and with the spoils enriched of nations. There the Capitol thou seest, above the rest lifting his stately head on the Tarpeian rock, her citadel impregnable; and there Mount Palatine, the imperial palace, compass huge, and high the structure, skill of noblest architects, with gilded battlements, conspicuous far, turrets, and terraces, and glittering spires.

"Many a fair edifice besides, more like houses of gods– so well I have disposed my aerie microscope– **Thou** may'st behold, outside and inside both, pillars and roofs carved work, the hand of famed artificers in cedar, marble, ivory, or gold. Thence to the gates cast round **Thine** eye, and see what conflux issuing forth, or entering in: praetors, proconsuls to their provinces hasting, or on return, in robes of state; lictors and rods, the ensigns of their power; legions and cohorts, turms of horse and wings; or embassies from regions far remote, in various habits, on the Appian road, or on the AEmilian– some from farthest south, Syene, and where the shadow both way falls, meroe, Nilotic isle, and, more to west, the realm of Bocchus to the Blackmoor sea; from the Asian kings (and Parthian among these), from India and the Golden Chersoness, and utmost Indian isle Taprobane, dusk faces with white silken turbants wreathed; from Gallia, Gades, and the British west; Germans, and Scythians, and Sarmatians north beyond Danubius to the Tauric pool.

¶ "All nations now to Rome obedience pay– to Rome's great Emperor, whose wide domain, in ample territory, wealth and power, civility of manners, arts and arms, and long renown, **Thou** justly may'st prefer before the Parthian. These two thrones except, the rest are barbarous, and scarce worth the sight, shared among petty kings too far removed; these having shewn thee, I have shewn **Thee** all the kingdoms of the world, and all their glory. This Emperor hath no son, and now is old, old and lascivious, and from Rome retired to Capreae, an island small but strong on the Campanian shore, with purpose there his horrid lusts in private to enjoy; committing to a wicked favourite all public cares, and yet of him suspicious; hated of all, and hating.

"With what ease, endued with regal virtues as thou art, appearing, and beginning noble deeds, might'st **Thou** expel this monster from his throne, now made a sty, and, in his place ascending, a victor-people free from servile yoke! And with my help **Thou** may'st; to me the power is given, and by that right I give it **Thee**. Aim, therefore, at no less than all the world; aim at the highest; without the highest attained, will be for **Thee** no sitting, or not long, on David's throne, be prophesied what will."

But **He** instead prophesied a Prophecy, **"Speaketh thee of Prophecies? Come hither; I will shew unto thee the judgment of the great whore that sitteth upon many waters: with whom the kings of the earth have committed fornication, and the inhabitants of the earth have been made drunk with the wine of her fornication."**

So **He** carried Satan in the spirit into the wilderness: and the devil saw a woman sit upon a scarlet coloured beast, full of names of blasphemy, having seven heads and ten horns. And the woman was arrayed in purple and scarlet colour, and decked with gold and precious stones and pearls, having a golden cup in her hand full of abominations and filthiness of her fornication: And upon her forehead was a name written,

MYSTERY, BABYLON THE GREAT, THE MOTHER OF HAR-
LOTS AND ABOMINATIONS OF THE EARTH. And the devil
saw the woman drunken with the blood of the saints, and
with the blood of His martyrs: and when the devil saw her,
he wondered with great amazement at how He knew his
machinations.

And He said unto devil, "Wherefore didst thou marvel? I will tell thee the mystery of the woman, and of the
beast that carrieth her, which hath the seven heads and
ten horns. The beast that thou sawest was, and is not;
and shall ascend out of the bottomless pit, and go into
perdition: and they that dwell on the earth shall wonder,
whose names were not written in the book of life from
the foundation of the world, when they behold the beast
that was, and is not, and yet is.

"And here is the mind which hath wisdom. The
seven heads are seven mountains, on which the woman
sitteth. And there are seven kings: five are fallen, and one
is, and the other is not yet come; and when he cometh,
he must continue a short space. And the beast that was,
and is not, even he is the eighth, and is of the seven, and
goeth into perdition.

"And the ten horns which thou sawest are ten kings,
which have received no kingdom as yet; but receive power as kings one hour with the beast. These have one
mind, and shall give their power and strength unto the
beast. These shall make war with the Lamb, and the
Lamb shall overcome them: for He is Lord of lords,
and King of kings: and they that are with Him are
called, and chosen, and faithful

"The waters which thou sawest, where the
whore sitteth, are peoples, and multitudes, and
nations, and tongues. And the ten horns which

thou sawest upon the beast, these shall hate the whore, and shall make her desolate and naked, and shall eat her flesh, and burn her with fire. For God hath put in their hearts to fulfil his will, and to agree, and give their kingdom unto the beast, until the words of God shall be fulfilled. And the woman which thou sawest is that great city, which reigneth over the kings of the earth."

And He continued Prophesying Prophecies of the a forthcoming Prophet, "Babylon the great is fallen, is fallen, and is become the habitation of devils, and the hold of every foul spirit, and a cage of every unclean and hateful bird. For all nations have drunk of the wine of the wrath of her fornication, and the kings of the earth have committed fornication with her, and the merchants of the earth are waxed rich through the abundance of her delicacies.

"Come out of her, My people, that ye be not partakers of her sins, and that ye receive not of her plagues. For her sins have reached unto heaven, and God hath remembered her iniquities. Reward her even as she rewarded you, and double unto her double according to her works: in the cup which she hath filled fill to her double. How much she hath glorified herself, and lived deliciously, so much torment and sorrow give her: for she saith in her heart, I sit a queen, and am no widow, and shall see no sorrow. Therefore shall her plagues come in one day, death, and mourning, and famine; and she shall be utterly burned with fire: for strong is the LORD God who judgeth her.

"And the kings of the earth, who have committed fornication and lived deliciously with her, shall bewail her, and lament for her, when they shall see the smoke of her burning, standing afar off for the fear of her torment, saying, Alas, alas that great city Babylon, that mighty city! for in one hour is thy judgment come.

"And the merchants of the earth shall weep and mourn over her; for no man buyeth their merchandise any more: The merchandise of gold, and silver, and precious stones, and of pearls, and fine linen, and purple, and silk, and scarlet, and all thyine wood, and all manner vessels of ivory, and all manner vessels of most precious wood, and of brass, and iron, and marble, and cinnamon, and odours, and ointments, and frankincense, and wine, and oil, and fine flour, and wheat, and beasts, and sheep, and horses, and chariots, and slaves, and souls of men. And the fruits that thy soul lusted after are departed from thee, and all things which were dainty and goodly are departed from thee, and thou shalt find them no more at all. The merchants of these things, which were made rich by her, shall stand afar off for the fear of her torment, weeping and wailing, and saying, Alas, alas that great city, that was clothed in fine linen, and purple, and scarlet, and decked with gold, and precious stones, and pearls! For in one hour so great riches is come to nought. And every shipmaster, and all the company in ships, and sailors, and as many as trade by sea, stood afar off, and cried when they saw the smoke of her burning, saying, What city is like unto this great city!

"And they cast dust on their heads, and cried, weeping and wailing, saying, Alas, alas that great city, wherein were made rich all that had ships in the sea by reason of her costliness! for in one hour is she made desolate. Rejoice over her, thou heaven, and ye holy apostles and prophets; for God hath avenged you on her.

"Thus with violence shall that great city Babylon be thrown down, and shall be found no more at all. And the voice of harpers, and musicians, and of pipers, and trumpeters, shall be heard no more at all in thee; and no craftsman, of whatsoever craft he be, shall be found any more in thee; and the sound of a millstone shall be heard no more at all in thee; and the light of a candle shall shine no more at all in thee; and the voice of the bridegroom and of the bride shall be heard no more at all in thee: for thy merchants were the great men of the earth; for by thy sorceries were all nations deceived. And in her was found the blood of prophets, and of saints, and of all that were slain upon the earth."

He said, and stood; but Satan, smitten with amazement, fell. So Satan fell; and straight a fiery globe of Angels on full sail of wing flew nigh, who on their plumy vans received Him soft from His uneasy station, and upbore, as on a floating couch, through the blithe air; then, in a flowery valley, set Him down on a green bank, and set before Him spread a table of celestial food, divine ambrosial fruits fetched from the Tree of Life, and from the Fount of Life ambrosial drink, that soon refreshed Him wearied, and repaired what hunger, if aught hunger, had impaired, or thirst; and, as He fed, Angelic quires sung heavenly anthems of His victory over temptation.

Thus they the Son of God, our Saviour meek, sung victor, and, from heavenly feast refreshed, brought on his way with joy. He, unobserved, home to His mother's house private returned. ✝

Chapter 4
"The Unholy One of Satan"

**ND WHENTHEREFORE, THE** angels ministered had unto Him, and after Herod Antipas cast John into prison, He departed into Galilee; and leaving Nazareth, He came and dwelt in Capernaum, which is upon the sea coast, in the borders of Zabulon and Nephthalim. That it might be fulfilled which was spoken by Isaiah the prophet, saying:

"Nevertheless the dimness shall not be such as was in her vexation, when at the first he lightly afflicted the land of Zebulun and the land of Naphtali, and afterward did more grievously afflict her by the way of the sea, beyond Jordan, in Galilee of the nations. The people that walked in darkness have seen a great light: they that dwell in the land of the shadow of death, upon them hath the light shined.

46

"Thus saith God the LORD, he that created the heavens, and stretched them out; He that spread forth the earth, and that which cometh out of it; He that giveth breath unto the people upon it, and spirit to them that walk therein: 'I the LORD have called Thee in righteousness, and will hold Thine hand, and will keep Thee, and give Thee for a covenant of the people, for a light of the Gentiles; to open the blind eyes, to bring out the prisoners from the prison, and them that sit in darkness out of the prison house. I AM the LORD: that is My name: and My glory will I not give to another, neither My praise to graven images. Behold, the former things are come to pass, and new things do I declare: before they spring forth I tell You of them.' "

From that time He began to preach, and to say, "Repent: for the kingdom of heaven is at hand." And He, walking by the sea of Galilee, saw two brethren, Simon called Peter, and Andrew his brother, casting a net into the sea: for they were fishers. And He saith unto them, "Follow Me, and I will make you fishers of men." And they straightway left their nets, and followed Him. And going on from thence, He saw other two brethren, James the son of Zebedee, and John his brother, in a ship with Zebedee their father, mending their nets; and He called them. And they immediately left the ship and their father, and followed Him.

And they went into Capernaum, a city of Galilee; and straightway on the sabbath day He entered into the synagogue, and taught. And they were astonished at His doctrine: for He taught them as one that had authority, and not as the scribes. He taught, "But the Spirit of the Lord departed from Saul, and an evil spirit from the Lord troubled him. And Saul's servants said unto him, 'Behold now, an evil spirit from God troubleth thee. Let our lord now command thy servants, which are before thee, to seek out a man, who is a cunning player on an harp: and it shall come to pass, when the evil spirit from God is upon thee, that he shall play with his hand, and thou shalt be well.' And Saul said unto his servants, 'Provide me now a man that can play well, and bring him to me.'

"Then answered one of the servants, and said, 'Behold, I have seen a son of Jesse the Bethlehemite, that is cunning in playing, and a mighty valiant man, and a man of war, and prudent in matters, and a comely person, and the Lord is with him.' Wherefore Saul sent messengers unto Jesse, and said, 'Send me David thy son, which is with the sheep'. And Jesse took an ass laden with bread, and a bottle of wine, and a kid, and sent them by David his son unto Saul. And David came to Saul, and stood before him: and he loved him greatly; and he became his armourbearer.

"And Saul sent to Jesse, saying, 'Let David, I pray thee, stand before me; for he hath found favour in my sight.' And it came to pass, when the evil spirit from God was upon Saul, that David took an harp, and played with his hand: so Saul was refreshed, and was well, and the evil spirit departed from him."

And there was in their synagogue a man with an unclean spirit; and he cried out, saying, "Listen not to the elders and the chief priests and the scribes: I have great pride and take everlasting pleasure of my loins, they are accursed from Ye Christ these Thy brethren, Thy kinsmen according to the flesh: who are Israelites; to whom pertaineth the adoption, and the glory, and

King Saul and the exorcism by David, the harpist!

the covenants, and the giving of the law, and the service of God, and the promises; whose are the fathers, and of whom as concerning the flesh Christ came, who is over all, God blessed for ever.

"What more shall I say then? That the Gentiles, which followed not after righteousness, have attained to righteousness, even the righteousness which is of faith. But Israel, which followed after the law of righteousness, hath not attained to the law of righteousness. Wherefore? Because they sought it not by faith, but as it were by the works of the law. For they stumbled at that stumblingstone; as it is written, Behold, I lay in Zion a stumblingstone and rock of offence: and whosoever believeth on him shall not be ashamed. If authority you have, Jesus of Nazareth of the Galilee," said one of the scribes, "rebuke this blasphemer!"

And He stayed His hand and remained in silence.

"Let us alone; what have we to do with Thee, Thou Jesus of Nazareth?" the unclean spirit said. It saw not Him dressed in a coat without seam, woven from the top throughout but a glorious fuchsia cloak armed with a golden staff with the graven image of His crucifixion upon the headpiece. "Art Thou come to destroy us? I know Thee who Thou art, the Holy One of God."

A curious murmuring amongst the elders and the chief priest and the scribes buzzed like irritated bees, a murmuring of ignorance and folly. And the demoniac posed unto Him many questions, "Do they not know of the knowledge that God so loved the world, that He gave His only begotten Son, that whosoever believeth in Thee should not perish, but have everlasting life? Do they not know that God sent not His Son into the world to condemn the world; but that the world through Him might be saved? Do they not know that he that believeth on **Thee** is not condemned: but he that believeth not is condemned already, because he hath not believed in the name of the only begotten **Son of God**?

"Do they not know all things shall be subdued unto **Thee**, then shall the **Son** also **Thyself** be subject unto **Him** that put all things under **Him**, that **God** may be all in all? Have they not heard **Thy Father** saith, '**Thou art my Son, this day have I begotten Thee?**' And again, '**I will be to Him a Father, and He shall be to me a Son?**'

"Why therefore," the unclean spirit demandeth of **Him**, "Doth **God** harden their hearts, that **Thou** shall be crucified? Why must **Thee Christ** suffer for sins, the just for the unjust, that **Thou** might bring us to **God**, being put to death in the flesh, but quickened by the **Spirit**? Why is there no hope: but they will walk after our their devices, and their will every one do the imagination of his evil heart?

"Why should **Thy** disciples through the law am dead to the law, that they might live unto **God**? Art they crucified with **Thee**? Nevertheless they shall live; yet not they, but **Thee** liveth in them: and the life which they shalt live in the flesh they live by the faith of the **Son of God**, who loves them, and gave **Thyself** for them.

"Stand fast ye generation of vipers," the unclean spirit saith these things seeking to cripple the ministry and mission of **Him**, the unclean spirit knoweth **He** seeks to teach them, that the **Son of man** must suffer many things, and be rejected of the elders, and of the chief priests, and scribes, and be crucified, and after three days rise again, "Let this mind be in you, this is **Christ Jesus**: **Who**, being in the form of **God**, thought it not robbery to be equal with **God**: But made **Himself** of no reputation, and took upon **Him** the form of a servant, and made in the likeness of men: And being found in

fashion as a man, **He** humbled **Himself**, and became obedient unto death, even a death of the cross. Wherefore **God**
also hath highly exalted **Him**, and given **Him** a name which
is above every name: that at **Thy** name every knee should
bow, of things in heaven, and things in earth, and things
under the earth; and that every tongue should confess that
Thou art **Lord**, to the glory of **God the Father**.

"**Christ**!" the unclean spirit challenged, "Shall they
purge out therefore the old leaven, that **Thee** may be a new
lump, as **Thee** are unleavened. For even **Christ** should be
their passover sacrificed for them: therefore shall they keep
the feast, not with old leaven, neither with the leaven of
malice and wickedness; but with the unleavened bread of
sincerity and truth?

"Do they knoweth that the god of this world, my master and god, hath blinded the minds of them which believe
not, lest the light of the glorious gospel of **Christ**, who is
the image of **God**, should shine unto them?"

The unclean spirit caught a sickness in a burst of laughter and a quake came upon the synagogue, "Yea doubtless,
and I count all things due to their loss of the excellency of
the knowledge of **Christ Jesus the Lord**: for whom **Thy**
disciples shalt suffer the loss of all things, and do count
them but dung, that **Thy** disciples may win **Christ**!

"Wilt this generation pass not away until **Thee**, the
Lord Thyself, shall descend from heaven with a shout,
with the voice of the archangel, and with the trump of
God: and the dead in **Christ** shall rise first: then they
which are alive and remain shall be caught up together
with them in the clouds, to meet the **Lord** in the air:
and so shall we ever be with the **Lord**.

"Then cometh the end, when **Thou** shall have
delivered up the kingdom to **God**, even the **Father**;

when **Thou** shall have put down all rule and all authority and power. For **Thou** must reign, till **Thee** hath put all enemies under **Thy** feet. The last enemy that shall be destroyed is death."

And the elders and the chief priests and the scribes quaked at the words the unclean spirit, felt in the marrow of their bones that their names shalt not written in the book of life and be therefore cast into furnace of fire: there shall be wailing and gnashing of teeth. Were they not knowledgeable in the knowledge that the **LORD** shall punish the host of the high ones that are on high, and the kings of the earth upon the earth? And they shall be gathered together, as prisoners are gathered in the pit, and shall be shut up in the prison, and after many days shall they be visited?

"Ye generation of vipers, all," the unclean spirit saith to the elders and the chief priests and the scribes, "Look unto **Him** the author and finisher of your faith; who for the joy that was set before **Him** shalt endure the cross, despising the shame, and is set down at the right hand of the throne of **God**!"

And **He** rebuked him, saying, **"Hold thy peace, and come out of him."** And the unclean spirit had convulsed and his eyes abandoned their wells and withdrew into the depths of his skull, and flies and maggots came from this mouth and further he seized a dagger from his sash and split open his stomach lifting the flesh like unto opening a pouch and the stench of a tomb sickened them of the synagogue, hitherto his bowels gushed not out of his flesh for verily his viscera had decayed unto the grave. His heart beat not in his chest; his lungs breathed not the air; his stomach hungered not. Verily, he was the walking dead, and then the unclean spirit cried with a loud voice, the unclean spirit came out of him.

And then **He**, fearing not the devils which killed the man's body, but are not able to kill the soul: but rather fear **Him** which is able to which is able to destroy both soul and body in hell. When **He** called **His** twelve disciples together, and gave them power and authority over all devils, and to cure diseases: for all things are delivered unto **Him** of **His Father**: and no man knoweth the **Son**, but the **Father**; neither knoweth any man the **Father**, save the **Son**, and he to whomsoever the **Son** will reveal him. Wheretofore **He** then laid **His** hands on the dead whom walked and healed him of his disease which was death and the man goeth forth alive in the image of the **LORD**.

And they were all amazed, insomuch that they questioned among themselves, saying, "What thing is this? what new doctrine is this? for with authority commandeth **He** even the unclean spirits, and they do obey **Him**?" And immediately his fame spread abroad throughout all the region round about Galilee. ✠

Chapter 5
"Gadarene Swine"

EHOLD, THERE AROSE A GREAT tempest in the sea, insomuch that the waves covered the ship, seeking to drown the men in the midst of the cold seas: for the winds howled, the lightning flashed, the thundered bellowed, the hail slung its stones from the slings of the darkened clouds, the mast strained like the mightiest of trees, the winds sought to uproot it, the wood of the slats screamed in torment, the winds sought to rent the sails in twain not unlike the veil of the temple shalt be rent when He is crucified, and the men huddled together afeard of the deep.

But He slepted in the peace of the LORD though they increased that troublest Him! many are they that rise up against Him. Many there be which say of their soul, there is no help for Him in God. But Thou, O! LORD, art a shield for Him; His glory, and the lifter up of **His** head. **He** cries unto the **LORD** with **His** voice, and **He** heard **Him** out of **His** holy hill. **He** laid down and slept amisdst the tempest; when **He** awakens; the **LORD** shalt sustain **Him**. **He** is not afraid of ten thousands of people, that have set themselves against **Him** round about. Arise, O! **LORD**; save **Him**, O! my **God**: for **Thou** hast smitten all **His** enemies upon the cheek bone; **Thou** hast broken the teeth of the ungodly. Salvation belongeth unto the **LORD**: **Thy** blessing is upon **Thy** people.

Simon Peter, the rock on which **He** built **His** ship, afeard the anger of the **LORD**. The howling of the winds were the breathe of **God** that they should perish, and by the blast of his nostrils will they be consumed by the crashing waves for in the greatness of thine excellency should **God** overthrow them that rose up against **Thee**: **Thou** sends forth **Thy** wrath, which consume them as chaff. Was this the day of the **LORD** cometh, cruel both with wrath and fierce anger, to lay the land desolate: and **He** shall destroy the sinners thereof out of it?

Did not **He** came to Nazareth, where **He** had been brought up: and, as **His** custom, **He** went into the synagogue on the sabbath day, and stood up for to read. And there the elders delivered unto **Him** the book of the prophet Isaiah. And when **He** had opened the book, **He** found the place where it was written:

"The Spirit of the LORD is upon Me, because He hath anointed Me to preach the gospel to the poor; He hath sent Me to heal the brokenhearted, to preach deliverance to the captives, and recovering of sight to the blind, to set at liberty them that are bruised, to preach the acceptable year of the LORD."

Did **He** not close the book, and give it again to the minister, and sit down? Were not the eyes of all them that were in the synagogue fastened on **Him**. And when **He** began to say unto them, **"This day is this scripture fulfilled in your ears"**, did not all bare **Him** witness, and wondered at the gracious words which proceeded out of **His** mouth. Did they not say, "Is not this Joseph's son?"

And then proceeded **He** to saith unto them, **"Ye will surely say unto Me this proverb: Physician, heal thyself: whatsoever we have heard done in Capernaum, do also here in thy country."** And **He** said, **"Verily I say unto you, No prophet is accepted in his own country. But I tell you of a truth, many widows were in Israel in the days of Elias, when the heaven was shut up three years and six months, when great famine was throughout all the land; but unto none of them was Elias sent, save unto Sarepta, a city of Sidon, unto a woman that was a widow. And many lepers were in Israel in the time of Eliseus the prophet; and none of them was cleansed, saving Naaman the Syrian."**

Why then, Peter weighed, did **He** provoke all they in the synagogue, for when they heard these things, they were filled with wrath, and rose up, and thrust **Him** out of the city, and led **Him** unto the brow of the hill whereon they built their city, that they might cast **Him** down headlong? But **He** passing through the midst of them went **His** way,

Peter besought the **LORD** to why **He**, whom was the **Son of God**, was displeased and why **His** anger was kindled; and the breath of the **LORD** brought this tempest upon the seas so that the waters should consume them by breaking their ship and they should drown in the depts of the sea. Should he instead cry unto Moses; for when Moses prayed unto the **LORD**, the fire quenched as should this tempest of the seas be. Should he cut off his hair, O! **LORD God of Israel**, and cast it away, and take up a lamentation on high places; for

the LORD hath rejected His disciples and forsaken them of His wrath.

And John the disciple whom He loved, verily the water of the sea soaked through the flesh, his blood iced over the rivers of his veins, to his very bone to his very soul that shivered and shook as though He found him from his mid-breast in the ice at the very centre of Hell. John prayed a prayer of the Psalmist, "O! He is my shepherd; I shall not want. He maketh me to lie down in green pastures: He leadeth me beside the still waters. He restoreth my soul: He leadeth me in the paths of righteousness for His name's sake. Yea, though I walk through the valley of the shadow of death, I will fear no evil: for Thou art with me; Thy rod and Thy staff they comfort me. Thou preparest a table before me in the presence of mine enemies: Thou anointest my head with oil; my cup runneth over. Surely goodness and mercy shall follow me all the days of my life: and I will dwell in the house of the LORD for ever."

And the other of His disciples came to Him, and awoke Him, saying, "Lord, save us: or we shall perish. Be merciful unto us, O! Lord: for man would swallow me up; we fight daily those who oppresseth us. Our enemies would daily swallow us up: for they be many that fight against us, O! Thou most High. What time we are afraid, we will trust in Thee. In God we will praise Thy word, in Thee have we put our trust; we will not fear what flesh can do unto us. Every day they wrest our words: all our thoughts are against us for evil. We gather themselves together, we hide ourselves, we mark our steps, when we wait for our souls. Shall we escape by iniquity? in thine anger cast down the people, O! Lord. Thou tellest our wanderings: put Thou our tears into Thy bottle: are they not in

The calming of the seas!

Thy book? When we cry unto Thee, then shall our enemies
turn back: this we know; for God is for us. In God will we
praise His word: in the LORD will we praise His word.
In God have we put our trust: we will not be afraid what
man can do unto us. Thy vows are upon me, O! God: I will
render praises unto thee. For Thou hast delivered our souls
from death: wilt not Thou deliver our breathe from drowning, that we may walk before God in the light of the living?"

And He saith unto them, "Why are ye fearful, O! ye
of little faith?" Then He arose, and rebuked the winds and
the sea; and there a great calm came upon the waters that it
should be fulfilled the words of the Psalmist: "They that go
down to the sea in ships, that do business in great waters;
these see the works of the LORD, and His wonders in
the deep. For He commandeth, and raiseth the stormy
wind, which lifteth up the waves thereof. They mount
up to the heaven, they go down again to the depths: their
soul is melted because of trouble. They reel to and fro,
and stagger like a drunken man, and are at their wit's
end. Then they cry unto the LORD in their trouble, and
He bringeth them out of their distresses. He maketh the
storm a calm, so that the waves thereof are still."

But the men marvelled, saying, "What manner of Man
is this, that even the winds and the sea obey Him!" And
howbeit His spirit, sitting in the comfort of the ship, was
not calm. Now with the seas calm they believed not and
He shewed unto His disciples, how that He must go unto
Jerusalem, and suffer many things of the elders and chief
priests and scribes, and be killed, and be raised again,
the third day, they believed not and when He is crucified will they finally believe and then when He is
Resurrected, some amongst them will not believe,
yet because they hast seen Him, they hast believed:

blessed are they that have not seen, and yet have believed.

And they came over unto the other side of the sea, into the country of the Gadarenes. And when **He** cometh out of the ship, immediately there met **Him** out of the tombs a man with an unclean spirit, who ware no clothes, neither abode in any house, but in the tombs. The men of Gadara had often seized him, and kept him under guard, bound with chains and shackles; howbeit often he broke the bonds and the demon with him therefore drove him into the wilderness. Thereafter no man of Gadara could bind him, no, not with chains: because that he had been often bound with fetters and chains, and the chains had been plucked asunder by him, and the fetters broken in pieces: neither could any man tame him. And always, night and day, he abided in the mountains, and in the tombs, crying, and cutting himself with stones.

But when he saw **Him** afar off, he ran and worshipped **Him**, and cried with a loud voice, and said, "What have I to do with thee, **Jesus**, **Thou Son** of the most **high God**? I adjure **Thee** by **God**, that **Thou** torment me not. For **Thine** is the **Kingdom of Heaven**. Knoweth I do the knowledge that the **Lamb** shalt be slain, to receive power and riches and wisdom and strength and honor and glory and blessing! and that every (other) creature (than I) which is in heaven, and on the earth, and under the earth, and such as are in the sea, and all that are in them, is heard saying, 'Blessing, and honour, and glory, and power, be unto **Him** that sitteth upon the throne, and unto the **Lamb** for ever and ever.'

"For He said unto the other demoniac, "Come out of the man, thou unclean spirit.""

"Come out of the man?" the unclean spirit mocked with laughter and scorn, "What cometh out of this man? Me the unclean spirit? Knoweth I Thee once saith, 'That which cometh out of the man, that defileth the man. For from within, out of the heart of men, proceed evil thoughts, adulteries, fornications, murders, Thefts, covetousness, wickedness, deceit, lasciviousness, an evil eye, blasphemy, pride, foolishness: All these evil things come from within, and defile the man.' Is this man defiled in Thy eyes? Shalt Thee condemeth this man when I cometh out of him?

"I, one of the unrighteous, shall not inherit the Kingdom of Heaven. Knoweth I that neither fornicators, nor idolaters, nor adulterers, nor effeminate, nor abusers of themselves with mankind, nor thieves, nor covetous, nor drunkards, nor revilers, nor extortioners, shall inherit the Kingdom of Heaven. Nor do I so wish it. I attend the god of this world, whom hath opened the eyes of mine which believe not, lest the light of Thy glorious gospel, Who is the image of God, should enslave unto me.

And He asked him, "What is thy name?"

He compelled the unclean spirit to again answer, "My name is Asmodeus the Lustful!" And the Gadarenes murmured amongst themselves knowing finally the name of the demoniac, for all of the people possessed the knowledge that Solomon the Exorcist requested and required both knowing humbly his name and his business, to then cast the unclean spirit out. And heretofore He having taught in the synagogue knoweth this as well.

And the demoniac further saith, "My name is Beelzebub the Gluttonous! My name is the Envious

Leviathan! My name is Belphagor the Slothful! My name is the Greedy Mammon!" The Gadarenes comprehendeth not the nature of this creature, though **He** was not ignorant of his name, nor of the number of the unclean spirits where were in the man; but party that it might be known what a miserable condition this poor man was in, being infested and vexed with such a large company of devils; and partly, that his own pity and power in delivering him, might be more manifest[1].

"My name is Lucifer," the demoniac continued, "the son of morning, who cuts down to the ground and weakens the nations! My name Satan the Wrathful, the great dragon, that old serpent, call the Devil and **Thy** Tempter!"

And **He** asked once more of him, **"What is thy name?"**

And he answered, again saying, "My name is **Legion**: for we are *many!*" And **He** saith not, but instead commanded him, **"Come out of the man, thou unclean spirit!"** And Legion felt compelled to obey.

The Gadarenes their eyes turned from the scene and their ears covered to shield them from the convulsing seized the demoniac's muscles rent from his bones cracked and broken, distorting him into a trinity of unnatural forms. The first metamorphosis being like unto a dog onto four-legs with a chorus of howling ravenous wolves echoing across the wilderness and down into the city of Gadara. The second metamorphosis twisted and distorted the demonic into the likeness a desert scorpion with arms fractured into pincers and his legs backwards bent as the tail, striking at the townspeople with venomous toes. The third metamorphosis being like unto a bat when his hands tore at the flesh of his chest renting asunder flesh from bone, the cage of his ribs exposed, his heart

---

1 Gill, John, *Gill's Exposition of the Entire Bible*, Mark 5:9

pounded a drum-beat, his lungs screeched, the pitch maketh the dogs howl, forming wings, heretofore did the demonic abomination swoop down upon the screaming and scattering people to puck them with claw-like feet into the heights of the heavens, dropping them unto their deaths.

The painful shrieking of the legion of devils, divideth within the man into ten cohorts, each of six centuries, echoed through the tombs of Gadara, threatening to wake the dead. And afeard besought **Him** much that **He** would not send them all away out of the country.

Now there was there nigh unto the mountains a great herd of swine feeding and all the devils besought **Him**, saying, "Send us into the swine, that we may enter into them." And forthwith **He** gave them leave. And the unclean spirits went out, and entered into the swine: and the swine squealed knowing the knowledge they were possessed of unclean spirits and were to be choked in the sea. And the unclean spirits and the swine ran violently over a cliff into the sea, the swine were broken upon the rocks below, and their blood foamed in the surf of the shore, and all were choked in the sea.

And they that fed the swine fled, and told it in the city, and in the country. The Gadarenes went out to see what had been done to the demoniac. And they come to **Him**, and see him that the devil possessed, and had the legion, sitting, and clothed, and in his right mind: and they were afeard and angered concerning the thousands of most priceless swine destroyed over nothing! For these Galileans tended the great herd of swine feeding (they were about two thousand), though swine, but the **LORD** saith, if it divideth the hoof, yet cheweth not the cud, it is unclean unto you: ye shall not eat of their flesh, nor touch their dead carcase. For they in their greed tended the herd for the *Legio X Fretensis,* the Tenth Legion of the sea strait, in defiance of the Law and the will of the LORD.

And they that saw how it befell the mound of broken bones and asundered flesh and blood that remained of him that the Legion had possessed. The demoniac was then born again from the womb of gore bloodied, bones broken and viscera vivisected, born again of the flesh is but born of the flesh, and howbeit He seeketh that a man be born of water and of the Spirit, therefore he, whom is unclean no longer, cannot enter into the kingdom of God.

The unclean elders of Gadara began to pray Him to depart out of their coasts and saith, "This fellow doth not cast out devils, but by Beelzebub the prince of the devils." And He held his tongue for He knew their thoughts, yet He saith not these words though He possessed the desire, "Every kingdom divided against itself is brought to desolation; and every city or house divided against itself shall not stand: and if Satan cast out Satan, he is divided against himself; how shall then his kingdom stand? And if I by Beelzebub cast out devils, by whom do your children cast them out? therefore they shall be your judges. But if I cast out devils by the Spirit of God, then the kingdom of God is come unto you."

And when the man born of the womb of viscera cometh into the ship, he that had been possessed with the Legion prayed him that he might be with him. Howbeit He suffered him not, but saith unto him, "Go home to thy friends, and tell them how great things the Lord hath done for thee, and hath had compassion on thee" And he departed, and began to publish in Decapolis how great things He had done for him: and all men did marvel. ✝

Chapter 6
"The Boy Who Would Be Satan"

ASTERS!" A BE-GRIEVED FA-ther to a young child saith to **His** disciples, "I have come unto thee to maketh an appeal for my son, for the works of thy **Rabbi** art known from the Galilee, teaching in their synagogues, and preaching the gospel of the kingdom, and healing all manner of sickness and all manner of disease among the people, all the way to the city of David. My son hath a mute spirit; and wheresoever he taketh him, he teareth him: and he foameth, and gnasheth with his teeth, and pineth away. Vagrant exorcists stole from my purse with promises and maketh their spells in the name of Solomon the king, and blundered they did into a contest with a centurion in the army of Beelzebub, the Imperial Legate of devils, that they couldst not win. Heareth my pleas for I hear ye art disciples of the **Christ**, whom giveth unto ye the power against unclean spirits, to cast them out, and to heal all manner of sickness and all manner of disease."

And **His** disciples were overjoyed, and praised and glorified the **God** of heaven and earth. Once **His** disciples they hand tarried awhile in the bazaar of Jerusalem, and they had heard of a wise man, a prophet, nay! a **false prophet** of the **LORD**, whom possessed a little ring having a seal consisting of an engraved stone. And he said unto them, "Takest this ring, O! disciples of the **Christ**, king, son of David, the gift which the **Lord Sabaôth** has sent thee from Solomon, king, son of David. With it thou shalt lock up all the demons of the earth, and with their help thou shalt build up the kingdom of Heaven on earth. But thou must wear this seal of **God** and this engraving of the seal of the ring sent thee is a Pentalpha—"[1]

—And they paid handsomely from their purse, which Judas Iscariot kept as his obligation to his fellows. And the false prophet tooketh their coins and said, "Take this, and at the hour in which the demon shall come unto thee, throw this ring at the heart of the chest of the unclean one and say unto him 'In the name of **Lord Sabaôth** and **His** only begotten **Son**, the **Christ**, calls thee hither."

So **His** disciples took the ring, and went off unto the city of the father of the boy; and behold, the boy sat in the hearth of his home playing with a wooden wheeled ox, and according to the instructions received from the astrologer, they threw the ring at the heart of the chest of the child, and said, "**Lord Sabaôth** we call forth. Who art thou?" and the mute spirit within the boy spoke not, and they were disheartened because even they knew the knowledge that to cast out a devil ye

---

1   The Testament of Solomon, trans. by F.C. Conybeare, *Jewish Quarterly Review* Oct. 1898

needed his name. "Tell us, O! demon, to what zodiacal sign thou art subject? What star dost thou pass?" and the mute spirit within the boy again spoke not and they grew dejected. "Fear God, and tell us by what angel thou art frustrated?" and the mute spirit yet again spoke not and they were dispirited mightily. "Tell us the name of the fish which thou reverest"[1] and then the mute spirit within the boy screamed in strange silence and the boy thrashed about in feigned pain and in mock agony, insulting **His** disciples for lack of faith in their **Lord**:

For some of **His** disciples had sown, some of their seeds of faith fell by the way side, and the fowls of the air came and devoured it up; and some of their seeds fell on stony ground, where it had not much earth; and immediately it sprang up, because it had no depth of earth: but when the sun rose, it scorched; and because it had no root, it withered away. And some of their seeds fell among thorns, and the thorns grew up, and choked it, and it yielded no fruit. And **His** disciples prayed they had sown their seeds of faith fallen on good ground, and did yield fruit that sprang up and increased; and brought forth, some thirty, and some sixty, and some an hundred.

A great multitude about **His** disciples filled with wrath, and the scribes questioning with them as collaborators with Beelzebub. And **He** came into the city from in the midst of the wilderness and straightway all the people in the city and in the country, when they beheld **Him**, were greatly amazed, and running to **Him** saluted **Him** and worshipped **Him**. And **He** inquired of the scribes, **"What question ye have with them?"** And the scribes answereth, "Vagrant exorcists are they for they art not of the **LORD God of Israel**, but heathen idols worshipping a ring with arcane symbols. They hath Beelzebub, and by the prince of the devils casteth they out devils."

And **He** laughed a hearty laugh, **"How can Satan cast out Satan? And if a kingdom be divided against itself, that kingdom cannot stand. And if a house be divided against itself, that house cannot stand. And if Satan rise up against himself, and be divided, he cannot stand, but hath an end. No man can enter into a strong man's house, and spoil his goods, except he will first bind the strong man; and then he will spoil his house."**

And one of the multitude answered, the father of the unfortunate boy, and said, **"Master**, I have brought unto **Thee** my son, which hath a mute spirit; and wheresoever he taketh him, he teareth him: and he foameth, and gnasheth with his teeth, and pineth away: and I spake to **Thy** disciples that they should cast him out; and they could not."

And he asked his father, **"How long is it ago since this came unto him?"** And he said, "Since but a child. And ofttimes it hath cast him into the fire, and into the waters, to destroy him: but if **Thou** canst do any thing, have compassion on us, and help us."

He answereth him, and saith, **"O! faithless generation, how long shall I be with you? how long shall I suffer you? bring Me unto him."** And they brought **Him** unto the boy: and in the hearth of the home **He** saw not the boy and the father groweth in his concern and rebuked his wife in chastisement and the woman pointed towards the clay oven from which she and her daughters baketh their daily bread. The oven had been shaped by its creators into the form of a beehive and within the hellish hive, the boy sat upon stones heated with the hell-fire of the inferno. He cried not. The fire seared not. He bellowed not. The fire scorched not. He sat, on the hot coals, as a man would in prayer and supplication to the **LORD**, but this was not the **LORD**, but the **LORD**.

The eyes of the boy in stark white rolled into his head. And unclean spirit within the boy, who had been mute and spoke not a word, struggled with the tongue of the Galileans as if it were foreign and alien and stank of the Word of God, now with a great many words, choked and croaked a creed in vile mockery of Him and His Father and the Holy Ghost:

> I praise **Mighty and Merciless Satan**,
> **The Father of Lies**, O! despoiler of
> Heaven and earth. Despoiler of all things,
> Visible and invisible. I praise
> **The Prince of Darkness**, **the Son of Satan**,
> One of the many born of the Father
> Throughout all ages. **Darkness of Darkness.**
> **False God of False Gods**. Made not begotten.
> Never in substance with God the Father,
> Through whom all things are damned. Who for us men
> And for our damnation, **he** rose up from
> The pits of Hell. By the vulgar power
> Of the **Hounds of Hell**, was born of Lilith
> The Lustful and became a dæmon.
> **He** was betrayed by his own Creator,
> **He** suffered and was cast into the pits
> Of Hell. From the eighth day of Creation
> Until its End. In fulfillment of the
> Scriptures. **He** fell from Heaven and into
> Hell descended, and is seated at the
> Left hand of the Father of Lies. And **he**
> Will come again in damnation, to rule
> The living and the dead, And **his** kingdom
> There hath seen no end. O! I believe in
> **The Hounds of Hell**, **the Prince of Darkness**,
> The taker of life, who recedes with the
> **Father of Lies and the Prince of Darkness**.

With the **Father** and the **Prince**, **Satan** is
Worshipped and glorified. In one unholy,
Blasphemous and Satanic church. We praise
No baptism for the remission of
Glorious sin. I expect the defeat of
God in the coming war, the damnation in
Hell to come. I rebuke **the one false God**,
**The Father, the Impotent, Creator
Of Heaven and Hell**, and of all the things,
Importunate and insignificant.
I rebuke the **Bastard**, **Jesus the Christ**,
The only Son of God, eternally
Perverted of the **Father**, **God but not
God, Light but Darkness, False God from False God**
Created not begotten, nary in
Being with the **Father**. Though **Him** all things
Are damned. For us men, for our damnation,
He rose from the pits of Heav'n by the lusts
Of the **Holy Whoremonger**, **He** slimmed forth,
A fiery salamander, out of the
Unsullied cunt– Immaculate, Divine,
And Raped gash– of Mary the Virgin
Whore. **He** spewed like vomit and was born man.
For **His** cenobites' damnation shalt **He**
Be crucified by the Jews' pawn Pilate;
He shalt suffer the agony of our father
He shalt die not unlike a mongrel dog.
Shalt be buried a' stolen from the grave
By **His** Disciples and away hidden.
On the Third day **He** creeps from the shadows,
In nullification of the Scriptures.
Flee to the green pastures of Britain where
Shalt propagate the Line of David.
His heirs shalt come again, in condemnation,

To rule the living and demean the dead.
And the Church will come to a fitting end.
Yeah! I rebuke the **Holy Whoremonger**,
Their **Ghost**, **the Thief of Life**, who recedes from
The **Father** and from the **Bastard Son**.
The **Father** and the **Bastard Son**
And **He** is worshipped in idolatry.
He hast born false witness through the Prophets.
We rebuke the coming one holy and
Apostolic Church. Yeah! we rebuke one
Baptism for the forgiveness of sins.
We curse the resurrection of the dead
For no life abides in the world to come.

"Let us alone; what have we to do with thee, thou **Jesus of Nazareth**?" the unclean spirit saith in this wise. "Art **Thou** come to destroy us? I know **Thee** who **Thou** art, the **Holy One of God**."

He said unto him, **"If thou canst believe, all things are possible to him that believeth."** And straightway the father of the child cried out, and said with tears, "Lord, I believe; help **Thou** my unbelief."

When **He** saw that the people came running together, he rebuked the foul spirit, saying unto him, **"Thou once and now forever mute and deaf spirit, I charge thee, come out of him, and enter no more into him."** And the spirit cried, and rent him sore. And the boy undertook to crawl from the oven whereas the unclean spirit likewise crawled from the boy. But the unclean spirit would not let go of the boy with a price to be paid: the spirit's preternatural predilection for fire and burning coals protected the child no more.

The vision in the mind of the possessed boy during the The Dionicene Creed!

The hot coals and stones seared the hands and knees of the boy, who yelped and cried out for his mother. And the woman, his mother and his sisters and the woman of the village, wailed and wept greatly, gnashing their teeth and pulling out of their hair. And had the women heard elders and the chief priests and the scribes tell tales of terror of ancient sacrifices:

Could the scribes be truthful when they saith when Solomon was old, that his wives turned away his heart after other gods: and his heart was not perfect with the **LORD** his **God**, as was the heart of David his father. Solomon, king offered his sons and his daughters to the brass idol Molech, by worshipping its idol through immense offerings of fire which heated the idol to a glow and then, **"O! woe!"**, did Solomon take his sons and his daughters from the cradle of their mothers and laid the babe in the cradle of the arms of the idol. And did Solomon watch as the generous heat did scorch and sear the flesh of his children, crackling and charring of their flesh was a foul sound, and the stench of the sacrifice that arose to the heights of heaven. He worshipped not the **LORD** of his fathers before him, rather Solomon went after Ashtoreth the Goddess of the Zidonians, and after Milcom the abomination of the Ammonites. And Solomon did evil in the sight of the **LORD**, and went not fully after the **LORD**, as did David his father. Then did Solomon build an high place for Chemosh, the abomination of Moab, in the hill that is before Jerusalem, and for Molech, the abomination of the children of Ammon. And Solomon glorified Topheth, which is in the valley of the children of Hinnom.

   ¶ And the women hearing the foul sound of the crackling and charring of their boy's flesh in the very same oven they bake their daily bread, had a sudden enduring empathy for their ancient ancestors, those women whose children were seized from mothers' milk-breasts and sacrificed to now abandoned idols by priests seized with sacrilegious abandon. Knoweth them now the knowledge of why the scribes continueth to this very day warn the warning of the LORD:

"Again, thou shalt say to the children of Israel, Whosoever he be of the children of Israel, or of the strangers that sojourn in Israel, that giveth any of his seed unto Molech; he shall surely be put to death: the people of the land shall stone him with stones. And I will set My face against that man, and will cut him off from among his people; because he hath given of his seed unto Molech, to defile My sanctuary, and to profane My holy name. And if the people of the land do any ways hide their eyes from the man, when he giveth of his seed unto Molech, and kill him not: Then I will set my face against that man, and against his family, and will cut him off, and all that go a whoring after him, to commit whoredom with Molech, from among their people. And the soul that turneth after such as have familiar spirits, and after wizards, to go a whoring after them, I will even set my face against that soul, and will cut him off from among his people. Sanctify yourselves therefore, and be ye holy: for I AM the Lord your God. And ye shall keep my statutes, and do them: I am the Lord which sanctify you."

And the woman witnessed in their horror as this itinerant Rabbi, this vagrant exorcist, reached His hand into the oven to guide the child into His arms. But afrighted was the boy, who retreated further into the depths of the oven. The heat of the oven baked the flesh of the boy, charring and scarring his flesh with bursting blisters and roasting him alive. The stench of the young child, the perfume of death and decay, assaulted his family and his friends into sickness and bile. As He reached further and further into the afired oven, His own hand

baked in the high heat of the oven, with the stench of righteousness. Then the Holy Ghost came upon the boy to sooth
his wounds with the balm of grace. And the boy accepted
His hand and His embrace, and crawled from the oven. He
cradled the boy in his arms and swaddled him in His own
seamless robe, soothing the boy with a Psalm so much like
the lullabies sung by His mother when He was but a swaddling child:

"For Thou hast possessed My reins: Thou hast covered Me in My mother's womb. I will praise Thee; for I
am fearfully and wonderfully made: marvellous are Thy
works; and that My soul knoweth right well. My substance
was not hid from Thee, when I was made in secret, and
curiously wrought in the lowest parts of the earth. Thine
eyes did see My substance, yet being unperfect; and in Thy
book all My members were written, which in continuance
were fashioned, when as yet there was none of them."

He prayed over the boy, anointing him with the cook-
ing oil of olives, the prayer of faith saved the boy, and He
restored the flesh of the boy whole, like as he was before.

The boy who had been Satan then bounded off to play
with his brothers and his sisters and his friends remember-
ing not the agony of the oven, nor of the blasphemies the
unclean spirit uttered through his innocent mouth.

And when He cometh into the house, His disciples
asked him privately, "Why could not we cast him out?
Thou gaveth unto us power and authority over all devils
and to cure diseases!" And He said unto them, "Because
of your unbelief: for verily I say unto you, if ye have
faith as a grain of mustard seed, ye shall say unto this
mountain, 'Remove hence to yonder place'; and
it shall remove; and nothing shall be impossible unto you. But this kind goes not out but by
prayer and fasting."

Chapter 7
"The Mother of Harlots"

ARY OF MAGDALA, WHICH IS on the shore of the Sea of Galilee, was found to be swollen with child though she was not married, nor betrothed, and presumed always to be a virgin. Her father, being just man and beholden to the behest of her mother and her sisters, and not willing to make her a public example, minded to put her away privily. An angel of the **LORD** appeared to her father, in the guise of a prostitute, having put on the whole armour of the Devil, standing therefore having her loins girt about with fornication, and her feet shod with the preparation of the apocalypse, the veil of the rouge and lips-stain of the brothel, a lone sheath to bare the sword of adultery, and having on the gilded nipples of lust and lasciviousness upon her breast, saying, "Fear not to spare thy child Mary: for that which is conceived in

her is of the **Holy Ghost**", but Mary's father believed not the palpable fallen angel of the infernal lord. Her father, rightly, afeard that his child had been seduced by lecherous Devils in the night for she swelled with child to the point of birthing the child, if child it be, unnaturally within but a three cycles of the moon, and even had she issues, and her issue in her flesh be blood, and became unclean whilst perversely with child.

Mary the Magdalene had a sorrow because her hour cometh, when she should deliver the babe, but she cried in anguish, for there is no joy that a unclean spirit should been born into the world. She knoweth that one day the **LORD** himself will give Israel a sign and Behold! the virgin shall conceive and bear a son, and shall call his name Emmanuel, but her child's name is not Emmanuel, which being interpreted is, **God** with us, howbeit she was a virgin whom conceived and bear a son, and shall call his name instead Beelzebub, which being interpreted is, the Lord of the Flies.

Summoned to the house of her father were the midwives, to cries, to the wailing, to the shrieking of not only Mary, but her mother and her sisters and the midwives joined the chorus in lamentations of this unnatural labour, this perverse labour, a labour that was a blasphemy that mocked the very gift of life blessed unto the race of man by the **LORD God of Israel**. For man should be fruitful, and multiply, and replenish the earth, and subdue it: and have dominion over the fish of the sea, and over the fowl of the air, and over every living thing that moveth upon the earth, for Lo! children are an heritage of the **LORD**: and the fruit of the womb is his reward. Yet this birth was an abomination unto the **LORD**.

The learned of the Law amongst the elders

Mary Magdalene births a great red dragon! Salome the midwife loseth her hand!

of Magdala, whom stood outside the house, and amongst the midwives knew that once the sons of **God** had seen the daughters of men that they were fair; and they took them wives of all which they chose. There were once Nephilim, giants in the earth, in those days; and also after that, when the sons of **God**, whom like Lucifer, son of the morning, were fallen from heaven, came in unto the daughters of men, and they bare children to them, the same became mighty men which were of old, men of renown. The learned of the Law pondered, could it be that Mary of Magdala would bear a Nephilim in the present of days? And what could be done with the child of giants?

The widwives kept the elders and their stones at bay, for this was the work of women. Salome, the eldest of the midwives, inspected the crown of the child within Mary and withdrew her hand in terror and screaming and the wailing of the women witnessed her dismembered wrist which sought to release a flood of blood, howbeit was dammed by the seared and scorched and smoking flesh. And a woman fled the abode and sought **Him**, whom preached a sermon of good news on the side of a mount before the multitudes of Magdala. **He** abandoned **His** disciples instructing them to instead reiterate the Beatitudes to the multitudes so that **He** could heal this woman whom travailed at the command of the **LORD** that **He** will greatly multiply her sorrow and her conception; in sorrow she shalt bring forth children. **He** sorrowed for the woman of Magdala had hard labour.

As **He** entered the abode, then a deluge of her water issued forth from the wound of Mary and the measure of the issue brought a harrowing fright to the midwives whom wailed and wept and **He** then saw a beast rise up out of the sea of the water of the woman,

Salome the midwive loses her hand to the maw of the dragon!

having seven heads and ten horns, and upon his horns ten crowns, and upon his heads the name of blasphemy. And the beast which **He** saw was like unto a leopard, and his feet were as the feet of a bear, and his mouth as the mouth of a lion: and the Devil shalt give him his power, and his seat, and great authority. And **He** saw one of his heads as it were wounded to death; and his deadly wound was healed: and all the world wondered after the beast. And they worshipped the Devil which gave power unto the beast: and they worshipped the beast, saying, "Who is like unto the beast? who is able to make war with him?"

And there was given unto him a mouth speaking great things and blasphemies; and power was given unto him to continue forty and two months. And he opened his mouth in blasphemy against **God**, to blaspheme **His** name, and **His** tabernacle, and them that dwell in heaven. And it was given unto him to make war with the saints, and to overcome them: and power was given him over all kindreds, and tongues, and nations. And all that dwell upon the earth shall worship him, whose names are not written in the book of life of the Lamb slain from the foundation of the world.

And **He** saith unto the Beast, **"If any man have an ear, let him hear. He that leadeth into captivity shall go into captivity: he that killeth with the sword must be killed with the sword. Here is the patience and the faith of the saints."**

Then **He** beheld another beast coming up out of the earth of the abode of the family of Mary; and he had two horns like a lamb, and he spake as a dragon. And he exerciseth all the power of the first beast before him, and causeth the earth and them which dwell therein to worship the first beast, whose deadly wound was healed. And he doeth great wonders, so that he

maketh fire come down from heaven on the earth in the sight of men, and deceiveth them that dwell on the earth by the means of those miracles which he had power to do in the sight of the beast; saying to them that dwell on the earth, that they should make an image to the beast, which had the wound by a sword, and did live. And he had power to give life unto the image of the beast, that the image of the beast should both speak, and cause that as many as would not worship the image of the beast should be killed. And he causeth all, both small and great, rich and poor, free and bond, to receive a mark in their right hand, or in their foreheads: And that no man might buy or sell, save he that had the mark, or the name of the beast, or the number of his name.

And Mary saith with the voice of the Devil, "Here is wisdom, **Jesus of Nazareth, the Holy One of God.** Let him that hath understanding count the number of the beast: for it is the number of a man; and his number is Six hundred threescore and six."

Then **He** bore witness to this woman, Mary, giving birth unto a scarlet coloured beast which slithered and slimed from out between the thighs of the woman, full of names of blasphemy, having seven heads and ten horns. And Mary was suddenly and supernaturally now arrayed in purple and scarlet colour, and decked with gold and precious stones and pearls, having a golden cup in her hand full of abominations and filthiness of her fornication: the Caesar and the Senators queued from the seven hills of Rome to the hills of the Galilee in their enchantment, in their intoxication, in their avarice, in their lechery for the woman. The woman, whom the Devil carved in her blood upon her forehead, MYSTERY, BAB-YLON THE GREAT, THE MOTHER OF HAR-

LOTS AND ABOMINATIONS OF THE EARTH. The leaders of the nations of the earth know of their own knowledge that their lusts and lasciviousness in their adultery with the reviled Beguile of the Nile shalt soon turn to machinations and murderousness.

And **He** then saw Mary with the Grail, drunken with the blood of the saints, and with the blood of **His** martyrs, and they rutted and writhed betwixt her thighs longing and loathing the carnal knowledge she alone possessed bequeathed by the power of Pornè, the brothel goddess. While **He** gave them power against unclean spirits, to cast them out, and to heal all manner of sickness and all manner of disease and their ministry and apostleship to stand fast, and hold the traditions which their have been taught, whether by word, or the epistle, given unto them by prophecy with the laying on of the hands of the presbytery, howbeit they are fallen into forgetting forever **His** teachings for the lusts of worldly things. For **He** taught them: Love not the world, neither the things that are in the world. If any man love the world, the love of the **Father** is not in him. For all that is in the world, the lust of the flesh, and the lust of the eyes, and the pride of life, is not of the **Father**, but is of the world. And the world passeth away, and the lust thereof: but he that doeth the will of **God** abideth for ever.

Mary, who was enthralled by the Whore of Babylon, looked with craving into the **His** eyes as she spread her sultry thighs, yearning for **His** lusts to rise and **He** listened to the suffering and the cries of the saints and **His** martyrs as they died as she sought to seduce **Him** with the dragon's lies. And **He** rebuked the Whore of Babylon, saying, **"Hold thy peace, and come out of her."** And when the unclean spirit had torn her, and cried with a loud voice, the beast from the sea and the beast from the earth and the great dragon were cast out, that old serpent, called the Devil, and Satan, which deceiveth the whole world: and his angels were cast out of her with him.

And midwives and the elders of Magdala were all amazed, insomuch that they questioned among themselves, saying, "What thing is this? what new doctrine is this? for with authority commandeth he even the unclean spirits, and they do obey him." And immediately **His** fame spread abroad throughout all the region round about Galilee. ✝

Recieve Abandon All Hope, All Ye Who Enter Here

Imagine, if you will, there was a Gospel According to Stephen King or Neil Gaiman, the masters of horror and the macabre. Heretical? Blasphemous? _Why_ rewrite, reinterpret, and revolt the Gospels as Biblical Horror? _Can_ a horror novel be a Spiritual, Inspirational, and Transcendent religious experience? _Can_ horror be spiritually uplifting? _Can_ horror free you from sin? _Can_ horror inspire you to accept Jesus Christ as your Lord and Personal Saviour through suspense, mystery, terror, shock, and gore?

Yes!

Jesus Christ, born of the virgin Mary, suffered under Pontius Pilate, was crucified, died, and was buried. He descended into Hell to free the Biblical Patriarchs from bondage and then on the third day rise again from the dead. Only in this unique tome is the Harrowing of Hell a truly Transcendent horror _and_ religious experience!

Is _The Harrowing of the Inferno_ the perfect horror novel for you to read and keep you awake tonight?

- Are you a reader who dares read an absolutely unique novel: _both_ transcendent horror _and_ religious revelation?
- Are you a Christian who desires not only the inspiration of the Gospel, but truly experience the fear of God?
- Are you a horror aficionado who longs for exceptionally transcendent terror, horror, and revulsion?

Books also by Robert Dwight Brown

Satan's Preacher Man - Act 1
(ISBN 13: 978-1-931608-16-9)

The Complete King Delta Lyrics
(ISBN 13: 978-1-931608-19-0)

Orson Welles' Lost *War of the Worlds* **Screenplay**
(ISBN 13: 978-1-931608-23-7)

I Was A Teenage Angel of Death - An Unrequited Love Story
(ISBN 13: 978-1-931608-08-4)

The Holy Bible Trilogy: The Old, New & Next Testaments
(ISBN 13: 978-1-931608-49-7)

The Holy Bible Trilogy: The Crusadic Testament (editor)
(ISBN 13: 978-1-931608-50-3)

The Hauntings of Jeremiah & Ebenezer Scrooge (ISBN 13: 978-1-931608-43-5)

Orson Welles' Battle of *The War of the Worlds*:
Episode 1: The Day the Earth Misunderstood
(ISBN 13: 978-1-931608-46-6)

Alistair Strange and the Fan-Friction:
Original Ending **The War of the Words** (ISBN 13: 978-1-931608-58-9)
Alternate #1 **Make Love, Not War** (ISBN 13: 978-1-931608-67-1)
Alternate #2 **The Invisible Man** (ISBN 13: 978-1-931608-76-3)

The Gospels of Biblical Horror:
The Harrowed Heart (ISBN 13: 978-1-931608-48-0)
The First Exorcist / The Harrowing of the Inferno (ISBN 13: 978-1-931608-60-2)
The Machination of Vipers (ISBN 13: 978-1-931608-71-8)
The Machination of the Apostles (ISBN 13: 978-1-931608-55-8) *Coming Soon*™

Plays by Robert Dwight Brown†
The Gospel According to Shakespeare: The Passion
(ISBN 13: 978-1-931608-30-5)

Marquis de Sade's *A Midsummer Night's Wet Dream* *by Ophelia T'Wat*
(ISBN 13: 978-1-931608-36-7)

The Haunting of Jeremiah Scrooge /
The Haunting of Ebenezer Scrooge — Double Feature
(ISBN 13: 978-1-931608-47-3)

The Black Mass *by Sir Francis Dashwood*
(ISBN 13: 978-1-931608-37-4)

The Carols of the First Christmas
(ISBN 13: 978-1-931608-44-2)

ROBERT DWIGHT BROWN

The Harrowing of the Inferno

Dante's Inferno Remixed

FULL COLOR & ILLUSTRATED - RED LETTER EDITION
With the Words our Lord and Saviour in Red
& God the Father in Purple

Allonymous Books
A Division of Chi Xi Stigma Publishing Company, LLC

Dedicated to the Black Metal Gods
From Euronymous to Ihsahn & Samoth
To Abbath, Infernus, and ultimately Quorthon
Through your inspiration, I create my
Dark, Dreadful, and Dispiriting Gospel

Allonymous Books

A Division of Chi Xi Stigma Publishing Company, LLC

Trade Paperback— **ISBN 13: 978-1-931608-60-2**

Also Available: *The Harrowed Heart* — **ISBN 13: 978-1-931608-48-0**
Also Available: *The Machination of Vipers* — **ISBN 13: 978-1-931608-71-8**

Cover image: Bosch, Hieronymous, Follower of, *Christ in Limbo*, Indianapolis Museum of Art, Indianapolis, Indiana
Paper image:; http://www.myfreetextures.com/vintage-paper-texture-with-design/

The New Testament & Dante's Inferno Mixed:

The art of the remixing one artist's popular song by another artist/producer or the art of "sampling" in the hip-hop parlance of the late 1970's and 80's is lost on most people whom were not reared in the housing projects of the Bronx and other New York City boroughs. There block parties were hosted by the legendary likes of DJ Kool Herc, gave birth to an art-form predicated on the taking of the percussion "breaks" from one record and mixing it with the "breaks" of another record. This became known as sampling. As hip-hop evolved, so did the technology, allowing producers to take elements of various songs and mixing them together to make an entirely new song. This has proven to be highly controversial in the music industry (despite, or because of the profitability of the new work). The art of sampling continues to line the coffers of lawyers who argue the multitudinous lawsuits over copyright infringement. Where does one person's art (and property) end and another's art (and property) begin? That is one of the great questions raised by the rise of hip-hop.

Alan Moore's *The League of Extraordinary Gentlemen*, a series of comic-book miniseries, is a **remix (or sampling)** of literary main characters from novels *Dracula*, *King Solomon's Mines*, *20,000 Leagues Under the Sea*, *The Strange Case of Dr. Jekyll and Mr. Hyde*, *The Invisible Man*, *Orlando: A Biography*, and *Carnacki the Ghost-Finder* (all fallen into the public domain, conveniently).

The Holy Bible by its very structure is a literary **remix (or sampling)**. It's sixty-six books (according to Protestant Reformers) are each the individual works of human authors (howbeit a single divine Author). Each of the books stand on their own as individual works, but only when bound together into the **remix** called the Holy Bible, do they transcend the written word to become the Word of **God**.

The Old Testament is itself a **remix** of Hebrew oral and written

traditions and foreign mythologies. The Torah, once believed to be the work of a single author, namely Moses, is actually a **remix** of the independent authorships of the Jahwist, the Elohist, the Deuteronomist, and the Priestly sources. The other authors of the Old Testament took entire stories, prayers, and covenants from other older Hebrew scripture and freely inserted them into their own books, sometimes with nary a change to be found. Was this outright theft? Or was it a divine **remix**?

The New Testament is also an abuser of this type of divine literary **remix**. The Gospels of Matthew and Luke have been rightly accused by the most esteemed Biblical scholars over the centuries to have plagiarized wantonly the Gospel of Mark and the mysterious Q-"Gospel", creating three "synoptic" Gospels out of an original two (one having been forever lost to history). Only John's Gospel escapes this abuse of **remix** by writing an inherently original and at times throughout history, questioned Gospel. So much for originality.

Doubt me?

Choose any Study Bible worth its salt and you will discover a column of scriptural references for practically every verse in the entirety of the Old and New Testaments. While some of these references are merely thematic in nature, many are paraphrased and often direct quotations of other, older scripture. This is the nature of The Holy Bible: the Divine **Remix**.

Need I continue?

If Jesus, as many Atheists assert, was the fictional creation of his "followers", then the authors of the New Testament made the Gospel of "Jesus of Nazareth" a **remix** of the Messianic prophecies of their Hebrew scripture. If Jesus was either a historical person or the divine, then His ministry is a **remix** of Old Testament and wholly (Holy) original belief systems.

Could I take the texts of the Gospels of Matthew, Mark, Luke, and John and by cutting and pasting scriptures wantonly here and there, compose a truly original work? A horror novel?

Hell, yeah!

Doctrine or Doctored History:

I believe in God,
the Father almighty,
Creator of heaven and earth,

and in Jesus Christ, his only Son, our Lord,
who was conceived by the Holy Spirit,
born of the Virgin Mary,
suffered under Pontius Pilate,
was crucified, died and was buried;
he descended into hell;
on the third day he rose again from the dead;

This is a selection from the Apostles Creed *(Symbolum Apostolicum)*, and for well over a thousand years included not only the doctrine of the Holy Trinity, but another seemingly **insignificant belief** of the early Church, written of by St. Melito of Sardis, Tertullian, Hippolytus, Origen, and St. Ambrose, has been lost (mostly) to the sands of time: the Harrowing of Hell *(Descensus Christi ad Inferos)*.

If the Gnostic Gospels were written **"too late"** in the second century, then what about a medieval text (or my little volumes) called the *Gospel of Nicodemus* which includes a much, much earlier but mysterious *Acts of Pilate*, which includes the earliest and perhaps at one time canonical version of the *Descensus Christi ad Inferos*.

To Protestant Christians, who were not reared on the Roman Mass, where the Apostles Creed was recited (with Borg-like efficiency), the doctrine of the Harrowing of Hell is a complete mystery. While the Mormons do have a doctrine on the Harrowing of Hell, their particular and peculiar religion is a utter mystery to me.

To most modern Christians, Catholic or Protestant, the image of Hell that comes most readily to mind is Dante Alighieri's

The Inferno, the first part of 14th-century epic poem *The Divine Comedy*. The concept of the nine circles of Hell is probably unique with Dante. The concept of the apt agonies and poetic punishments for the sins of this life in the afterlife is not unique, because the Greek gods punished Sisyphus with the archetypal Sisyphean task of pushing a boulder up a steep hill, only to have it roll down to the bottom before it ever reached the summit. But Dante was far more interested in satirizing his contemporary and political rivals when he wrote *The Inferno* in exile from Florence.

My goal with *The Harrowing of the Inferno* was to marry the doctrine of the Harrowing of Hell and the archetypal Dante's *Inferno* into a single unified, for the modern audience, view of the *Descensus Christi ad Inferos*. Due to my penchant remixing the New Testament in the *The Harrowed Heart* and *The First Exorcist*, I wanted Jesus to encounter not only the patriarchs and prophets in the first circle of Hell, known as Limbo, but also through *all* of the other nine circles.

Why should some of the patriarchs and prophets rest peacefully in the Asphodel meadows of Limbo, only to be rescued by Jesus the Christ, when they were *guilty* of so many of the sins that Dante relished punishing his personal and political rivals in perpetuity. I very much *relish* the opportunity to punish the Old Testament patriarchs and prophets with apt agony and poetic punishment, drawing on the scripture itself in the *ultimate remix of not only the Old and New Testaments on the left turntable, but Dante's* Inferno *on the right, switching back and forth between the two, mixing the best beats, into a newer and greater work*: The Harrowing of the Inferno!

Circle 1
"The Asphodel Meadow"

IDWAY THROUGH THE JOUR-ney of our allotted life, and at the end of **His**, for the **LORD** hath given the days of our years at threescore years and ten; and if by reason of strength they be fourscore years, yet is our strength labour and sorrow; for it is soon cut off, and we fly away. But **He** was allotted a mere half of ours when crucified on the cross **He** was, yet accomplished more in **His** than any man before **Him** and after **Him** hath accomplished in ours:

Wherefore when **He** cometh into the world, **He** saith, **"Sacrifice and offering Thou wouldest not, but a body hast Thou prepared Me: in burnt offerings and sacrifices for sin Thou hast had no pleasure. Then said I, 'Lo! I come (in the volume of the book it is written of Me,) to do thy will, O! God.' "** Above when **He** said, **"Sacrifice**

1

Dante Alighieri, *The Inferno*, translated by Henry Wadsworth Longfellow (1867),
& abridged, adapted from, and expanded by Robert Dwight Brown

and offering and burnt offerings and offering for sin thou wouldest not, neither hadst pleasure therein"; which are offered by the Law; then said He, "Lo! I come to do Thy will, O! God." He taketh away the first, that He may establish the second. By the which will we are sanctified through the offering of His body of once for all. But when the fulness of the time was come, God sent forth His Son, made of a woman, made under the Law. He hath redeemed us from the curse of the law, being made a curse for us: for it is written, "His body shall not remain all night upon the tree, but thou shalt in any wise bury Him that day; (for he that is hanged is accursed of God;) that thy land be not defiled, which the LORD thy God giveth thee for an inheritance." For He also hath once suffered for sins, the just for the unjust, that he might bring us to God, being put to death in the flesh, but quickened by the Spirit and all we like sheep have gone astray; we have turned every one to His own way; and the LORD hath laid on Him the iniquity of us all.

For God hath made Him to be sin for us, who knew no sin; that we might be made the righteousness of God in Him. For God delivered unto us first of all that which He also received, how that He died for our sins according to the scriptures; and that He was buried, and that He rose again the third day according to the scriptures. Who is He that condemneth? It is He that died, yea rather, that is risen again, who is even at the right hand of God, who also maketh intercession for us. For He is not entered into the holy places made with hands, which are the figures of the true; but into heaven itself, now to appear in the presence of God for us: for to this end He both died, descended into Hades, and rose, and revived, that He might be Lord both of the dead and living. But why dost thou judge thy brother? or

why dost thou set at nought thy brother? for we shall all stand before **His** judgment seat. For if **God** spared not the angels that sinned, but cast them down to Hades, and delivered them into chains of darkness, to be reserved unto **His** judgment!

And a man came into the Asphodel Meadows carrying his own severed head upon a silver charger, and he was inquired of by all of the patriarchs and the prophets of the land of Israel: "Who art thou?" And the head sitting upon the charge answered them and saith: "I am John, the voice of one crying in the wilderness," and Isaiah, whom sat contemplatively under a tree, took notice, and saith unto John, "Are thee the voice of him that crieth in the wilderness, 'Prepare ye the way of the **LORD**, make straight in the desert a highway for our God"? And John answereth, "Yay! I am said voice of one crying in the wilderness." And Isaiah rejoiced, "Every valley shall be exalted, and every mountain and hill shall be made low: and the crooked shall be made straight, and the rough places plain: and the glory of the **LORD** shall be revealed, and all flesh shall see it together: for the mouth of the **LORD** hath spoken it."

"I am the prophet of the most **High**," John saith, "which came before the face of **His** advent to prepare **His** ways, to give knowledge of salvation unto **His** people, for the remission of their sins. And when I saw **Him** coming unto me, being moved of the **Spirit**, I beheld the **Lamb of God**, which taketh away the sin of the world. For after me cometh a **Man** which is preferred before me: for **He**

was before me. And I knew **Him** not: but that **He** should be made manifest to Israel, therefore am I come baptizing with water. And I saw the **Spirit** descending from heaven like a dove, and it abode upon **Him** and lo! a voice from heaven, saying, **'This is My beloved Son, in whom I AM well pleased.'** Howebeit, I knew **Him** not: but **He** that sent me to baptize with water, the same said unto me, **'Upon whom thou shalt see the Spirit descending, and remaining on Him, the same is He which baptizeth with the Holy Ghost.'** ”

Then Malachi came all the nearer to hear and upon his hearing, he proclaimed, “Behold, **I** will send you Elijah the prophet before the coming of the great and dreadful day of the **LORD**: and he shall turn the heart of the fathers to the children, and the heart of the children to their fathers, lest **I** come and smite the earth with a curse!”

And Isaiah proclaimed to all of the patriarchs and the prophets, “For unto the living a child has been born, unto them a **Son** has been given: and the government shall be upon **His** shoulder: and **His** name shall be called **Wonderful**, **Counsellor**, **The Mighty God**, **The Everlasting Father**, **The Prince of Peace**. Of the increase of **His** government and peace there shall be no end, upon the throne of David, and upon **His** kingdom, to order it, and to establish it with judgment and with justice from henceforth even for ever. The zeal of the **LORD** of hosts will perform this.”

So Jeremiah wept in his lamentations for the slain children of Bethlehem for hath saith the **LORD**, **“A voice was heard in Ramah, lamentation, and bitter weeping; Rahel weeping for her children refused to be comforted for her children, because they were not.”**

The dead knew not the time of the world for **His** ministry had not only began, howbeit, the **Son of man** already

had been betrayed into the hands of men: and they hath killed **Him**, and on the morrow, being the third day, **He** shall be raised again. The patriarchs and the prophets sought their inquiries with the Baptizer, Isaiah first asked in the fulfilment of his prophecies had come to pass, "Were the eyes of the blind opened, and the ears of the deaf art unstopped? Did the lame men leap as an hart, and the tongue of the dumb sing: for in the wilderness shall waters break out, and streams in the desert?" and John replied, "They were."

Then Zechariah asked in a similar vein, "Did thy **King** cometh unto Jerusalem? Is **He** just, and having salvation; lowly, and riding upon an ass, and upon a colt the foal of an ass?" and John saith, "**He** did and **He** was and **He** did."

And Jeremiah inquired of John, "Did **He** make a new covenant with the house of Israel, and with the house of Judah?" and John saith, "**He** did."

So the patriarchs and the prophets suddenly overwhelmed with wailing and the gnashing of teeth for they knew the knowledge of what John would soon proclaim. And a patriarch hesitantly asketh, though he wished he would not be made aware of the answer for it afrighted him, "For it was not an enemy that reproaches **Him**; then **He** could have borne it: neither was it he that hated **Him** that did magnify himself against **Him**; then **He** would have hid **Himself** from him: but it was a man of **His** equal, **His** guide, and **His** acquaintance. They took sweet counsel together, and walked unto the house of **God** in company. Was **He** betrayed by a friend?" and John saith, "**He** was."

Then tearfully Zechariah inquired, "The **LORD** once said unto me, '**Cast it unto the potter: a goodly price that I was prised at of them. And I took the thirty pieces of silver, and cast them to the potter in the house of the**

LORD.' Was He purchased for the price of thirty pieces of silver? and was the shepherd smitten, and the sheep scattered?" and John saith, "He was and they were."

And Isaiah begged of John through his tears, "Did He give His back to the smiters, and His cheeks to them that plucked off the hair: did He hide not His face from shame and spitting? Was He divided the spoils with the strong; because He hath poured out His soul unto death: and He was numbered with the transgressors; and He bare the sin of many, and made intercession for the transgressors?" and John saith, "He was."

Then Zechariah sought sobbing, "Were the inhabitants of Jerusalem, the spirit of grace and of supplications, looking upon Him whom they have pierced? And did they mourn for Him, as one mourneth for His only Son, and shall be in bitterness for him, as one that is in bitterness for His firstborn?" and John saith, "They did."

So then a patriarch beseeched with weeping and lamentation, "Was His body allowed to remain all night upon the tree, but shalt they in any wise bury Him that day (for he that is hanged is accursed of God)?" and John replied "His body was not."

At the last a last patriarch sought with expectations of glory and redemption, "Has the LORD set always before Him: because He is at His right hand, He shall not be moved? Therefore is His heart glad, and His glory rejoiceth: His flesh also shall rest in hope? Wilt He not leave His soul in Hades; neither wilt Thou suffer Thine Holy One to see corruption? Wilt He shew Him the path of life: in His presence is fulness of joy; at His right hand there are pleasures for evermore?" and John saith, "On the morrow, in very early in the morning the first day of the week, at the rising

of the sun, **He** shall be!

"By which also **He** shalt come and preach unto the spirits in prison; which sometime were disobedient, when once the longsuffering of **God** waited in the days of Noah, while the ark was a preparing, wherein few, that is, eight souls were saved by water!"

And the patriarchs and the prophets rejoiced greatly in celebration and praise of the **LORD**, and John saith, "But unto every one of us is given grace according to the measure of **His** gift. Wherefore **He** saith, "Thou hast ascended on high, Thou hast led captivity captive: Thou hast received gifts for men; yea, for the rebellious also, that the LORD God might dwell among them." Now that **He** must ascend, what is it but that **He** also must descend first into the lower parts of the earth? He that must descend is the same also that must ascend up far above all heavens, that **He** shalt fulfil all things!"

And **He** and **His** mute companion entered the deep and savage way and written on the summit of a gate were these words in sombre colour:

> THROUGH ME THE WAY IS TO THE CITY DOLENT;
> THROUGH ME THE WAY IS TO ETERNAL DOLE;
> THROUGH ME THE WAY AMONG THE PEOPLE LOST.
>
> JUSTICE INCITED MY SUBLIME CREATOR;
> CREATED ME DIVINE OMNIPOTENCE,
> THE HIGHEST WISDOM AND THE PRIMAL LOVE.

BEFORE ME THERE WERE NO CREATED THINGS,
ONLY ETERNE, AND I ETERNAL LAST.
ABANDON ALL HOPE, ALL YE WHO ENTER!

And then **He** scrawled, defacing the sign with graffiti so it now read, "RECEIVE ALL HOPE, FROM ME WHO ENTERS HEREIN!"

And the patriarchs and the prophets celebrated the coming of the **Messiah** as the voice in the wilderness had revealed unto them. And then came a certain man into the Asphodel Meadows, the brother of Mary and her sister Martha, whom had been sick. The sisters of the sick man, Lazarus of Bethany, had sent unto their **Rabbi** a message saying, "**Lord**, he whom **Thou** lovest is sick." And Lazarus understood not why he abode two days still in the same place where he was.

And John came unto Lazarus and saith, "When **He** received the message, **He** saith unto disciples, **'Our friend Lazarus sleepeth; but I go, that I may awake him out of sleep.'** Then said **His** disciples, '**Lord**, if he sleep, he shall do well.' Howbeit **He** spake of thy death: but they thought that **He** had spoken of taking of rest in sleep. Then said **He** unto them plainly, **'Lazarus is dead.'** "

And Lazarus collapsed amongst the asphodel and wept knowing that the eyes of the blind hath been opened, and the ears of the deaf hath been unstopped. And the lame man leapt as an hart, and the tongue of the dumb sang: for in the wilderness shall waters break out, and streams in the

desert. "Why did He not come when we called upon Him? Did He not heal the Centurion's servant, a Gentile whom believed? Was He not sought by one of the rules of the synagogue to heal his little daughter whom lieth at the point of death? Lord, if Thou hadst been here, I wouldst not have died. Why have I entered unto death and buried?"

And John asketh, "Do you believe He is the resurrection, and the life: he that believeth in Him, though he were dead, yet shall he live: and whosoever liveth and believeth in Him shall never die. Believest thou this?" Lazarus saith unto John, "Yea, prophet: I believe that He is the Christ, the Son of God, which should come into the world."

And unbeknownst to those in the Asphodel Meadows, when Martha, as soon as she heard that He was coming, went and met Him: but Mary sat still in the house. Then Mary buffeted Him with her hands and clawed at His face for her grief had made her wrathful. If she had had the strength she would have slew Him where he stood in the country of Bethany. If only she had a dagger to cut His heart out of His heartless chest and maketh Him a burnt offering unto His cruel Father. If only she had a noose, she would have hanged Him from a tree, for she knew from His own teaching that: cursed is every one that hangeth on a tree. And in her weeping, she said unto Him, "Lord, if thou hadst been here, my brother had not died. But I know, that even now, whatsoever thou wilt ask of God, God will give it Thee." He saith unto her, "Thy brother shall rise again." Martha saith unto Him, "I know that he shall rise again in the resurrection at the last day." He said unto her, "I AM the resurrection, and the life: he that believeth in Me, though he were dead, yet shall he live: and whosoever liveth and believeth in Me shall never die. Believest thou

this?" She saith unto him, "Yea, **Lord**: I believe that **Thou** art the **Christ**, the **Son of God**, which should come into the world."

And when she had so said, she went her way, and called Mary her sister secretly, saying, "The **Master** is come, and calleth for thee." As soon as she heard that, she arose quickly, and came unto **Him**. Now **He** was not yet come into the town, but was in that place where Martha met **Him**. The Jews then which were with her in the house, and comforted her, when they saw Mary, that she rose up hastily and went out, followed her, saying, "She goeth unto the grave to weep there." Then when Mary was come where **He** was, and saw **Him**, she fell down at **His** feet, saying unto him, "**Lord**, if thou hadst been here, my brother had not died."

When **He** therefore saw Mary, the sister of Lazarus weeping, and the Jews also weeping which came with her, **He** groaned in the spirit, and was troubled. And **He** said, **"Where have ye laid him?"** They said unto **Him**, "**Lord**, come and see." And **He** wept. And some of them said, "Could not this man, which opened the eyes of the blind, have caused that even this man should not have died?"

He therefore again groaning in **Himself** cometh to the grave. It was a cave, and a stone lay upon it. **He** said, **"Take ye away the stone."** Martha, the sister of him that was dead, saith unto him, "**Lord**, by this time he stinketh: for he hath been dead four days." Jesus saith unto her, **"Said I not unto thee, that, if thou wouldest believe, thou shouldest see the glory of God?"** Then they took away the stone from the place where the dead was laid. And **He** lifted up **His** eyes, and said, **"Father, I thank Thee that Thou hast heard Me. And I knew that Thou hearest Me always: but because of**

He *raises Lazarus from the dead, stealing him from the Asphodel Meadows!*

the people which stand by I said it, that they may believe that thou hast sent Me." And when He thus had spoken, he cried with a loud voice "Lazarus, come forth."

And in the Asphodel Meadows, Lazarus buckled over in pain and coughed and vomited forth a black mass from his innards, to the awe and astonishment of the patriarchs and the prophets, and then Lazarus faded before their eyes— And he that was dead came forth, bound hand and foot with graveclothes: and his face was bound about with a napkin. He saith unto them, "Loose him, and let him go."

Then John collapsed onto the soft grass and the asphodel overcome with overwhelming grief, his breath even in death was stolen from him, for he knoweth that the many of the Jews which came to Mary, sister of Martha and of Lazarus, and had seen the things which He did, believed on Him. But some of them went their ways to the Pharisees, and told them what things He had done. Then gathered the chief priests and the Pharisees a council, and said, "What do we? for this man doeth many miracles. If we let Him thus alone, all men will believe on Him: and the Romans shall come and take away both our place and nation."

And John saw one of them, named Caiaphas, being the high priest that same year, said unto them, "Ye know nothing at all, nor consider that it is expedient for us, that one man should die for the people, and that the whole nation perish not." And this spake he not of himself: but being high priest that year, he prophesied that He should die for that nation; and not for that nation only, but that also he should gather together in one the children of God that were scattered abroad.

Then from that day forth they took counsel together for to put Him to death. He therefore walked no more

openly among the Jews; but went thence unto a country near to the wilderness, into a city called Ephraim,
and there continued with His disciples.

And John knew the Jews' passover was nigh at
hand: and many went out of the country up to Jerusalem
before the passover, to purify themselves. Then sought
they for He, and spake among themselves, as they stood
in the temple, "What think ye, that He will not come to
the feast?" Now both the chief priests and the Pharisees had
given a commandment, that, if any man knew where He
were, he should shew it, that they might take Him.

And the patriarchs and the prophets were in this wise
their cries risen into a chorus of lamentations and Isaiah
stood upon a large stone and solemnly prayed his own
prophecy knoweth to the Jews and the disciples and those
that will come after them all as the suffering of the servant:

"Who hath believed our report? and to whom is the
arm of the LORD revealed? For He shall grow up before
Him as a tender plant, and as a root out of a dry ground:
He hath no form nor comeliness; and when we shall see
Him, there is no beauty that we should desire Him. He
is despised and rejected of men; a man of sorrows, and ac-
quainted with grief: and we hid as it were our faces from
Him; He is despised, and we esteemed Him not.

"Surely He shalt bear our griefs, and carry our sorrows: yet we did esteem Him stricken, smitten of God, and
afflicted. But He shalt be wounded for our transgressions,
He shalt be bruised for our iniquities: the chastisement of
our peace shalt be upon Him; and with His stripes we are
healed. All we like sheep have gone astray; we have turned
every one to his own way; and the LORD hath laid on Him
the iniquity of us all.

"He shalt be oppressed, and He shalt be afflicted, yet

He opens not His mouth: He shalt be brought as a lamb to the slaughter, and as a sheep before her shearers is dumb, so He shalt open not his mouth. He shalt be taken from prison and from judgment: and who shall declare His generation? for He shalt be cut off out of the land of the living: for the transgression of my people was He stricken. And He shalt make His grave with the wicked, and with the rich in His death; because He had done no violence, neither was any deceit in His mouth.

"Yet it pleased the LORD to bruise Him; He shalt put Him to grief: when Thou shalt make His soul an offering for sin, He shall see His seed, He shall prolong His days, and the pleasure of the LORD shall prosper in LORD hand. He shall see of the travail of His soul, and shall be satisfied: by His knowledge shall my righteous servant justify many; for He shall bear their iniquities. Therefore will I divide Him a portion with the great, and He shall divide the spoil with the strong; because He hath poured out His soul unto death: and He was numbered with the transgressors; and He bare the sin of many, and made intercession for the transgressors."

And He ascended not up on high, but that He also descended first into the lower parts of the earth. He that descends is the same also that shall ascend up far above all heavens, that He might fill all thing. So that He can lead captivity captive, and give gifts unto men, because unto every one of us is given grace according to the measure of the gift of Christ.

By which also **He** cometh now to preach unto the patriarchs and prophets in prison; which sometime were disobedient, when once the longsuffering of God waited in the days of Noah, while the ark was a preparing, wherein few, that is, eight souls were saved by water; by the blood of **His** covenant **He** hath sent forth **His** prisoners out of the pit wherein is no water.

And Isaiah stepped towards **Him** as if to remind himself that: "The earth shall reel to and fro like a drunkard, and shall be removed like a cottage; and the transgression thereof shall be heavy upon it; and it shall fall, and not rise again. And it shall come to pass in that day, that the **LORD** shall punish the host of the high ones that are on high, and the kings of the earth upon the earth. And they shall be gathered together, as prisoners are gathered in the pit, and shall be shut up in the prison, and after many days shall they be visited. Then the moon shall be confounded, and the sun ashamed, when the **LORD of hosts** shall reign in mount Zion, and in Jerusalem, and before **His** ancients gloriously."

Hence **He** preached unto and accepted the patriarchs and prophets into **His** Communion: for faith is the substance of things hoped for, the evidence of things not seen. For by it the elders obtained a good report. Through faith we understand that the worlds were framed by the word of **God**, so that things which are seen were not made of things which do appear.

By faith Abel offered unto **God** a more excellent sacrifice than Cain, by which he obtained witness that he was righteous, **God** testifying of his gifts: and by it he being dead yet speaketh.

By faith Enoch was translated that he should not see death; and was not found, because **God** had translated him: for before his translation he had this testimony, that he

pleased God. But without faith it is impossible to please him: for he that cometh to God must believe that he is, and that he is a rewarder of them that diligently seek him.

By faith Noah, being warned of God of things not seen as yet, moved with fear, prepared an ark to the saving of his house; by the which he condemned the world, and became heir of the righteousness which is by faith.

By faith Abraham, when he was called to go out into a place which he should after receive for an inheritance, obeyed; and he went out, not knowing whither he went. By faith he sojourned in the land of promise, as in a strange country, dwelling in tabernacles with Isaac and Jacob, the heirs with him of the same promise: for he looked for a city which hath foundations, whose builder and maker is God. Through faith also Sara herself received strength to conceive seed, and was delivered of a child when she was past age, because she judged him faithful who had promised. Therefore sprang there even of one, and him as good as dead, so many as the stars of the sky in multitude, and as the sand which is by the sea shore innumerable.

These all died in faith, not having received the promises, but having seen them afar off, and were persuaded of them, and embraced them, and confessed that they were strangers and pilgrims on the earth. For they that say such things declare plainly that they seek a country. And truly, if they had been mindful of that country from whence they came out, they might have had opportunity to have returned. But now they desire a better country, that is, an heavenly: wherefore God is not ashamed to be called their God: for he hath prepared for them a city.

By faith Abraham, when he was tried, offered up Isaac: and he that had received the promises offered up his only

begotten son, of whom it was said, that in Isaac shall thy seed be called: accounting that God was able to raise him up, even from the dead; from whence also he received him in a figure.

By faith Isaac blessed Jacob and Esau concerning things to come. By faith Jacob, when he was a dying, blessed both the sons of Joseph; and worshipped, leaning upon the top of his staff. By faith Joseph, when he died, made mention of the departing of the children of Israel; and gave commandment concerning his bones.

By faith Moses, when he was born, was hid three months of his parents, because they saw he was a proper child; and they were not afraid of the king's commandment. By faith Moses, when he was come to years, refused to be called the son of Pharaoh's daughter; choosing rather to suffer affliction with the people of God, than to enjoy the pleasures of sin for a season; esteeming the reproach of Him greater riches than the treasures in Egypt: for he had respect unto the recompence of the reward. By faith he forsook Egypt, not fearing the wrath of the king: for he endured, as seeing him who is invisible. Through faith he kept the passover, and the sprinkling of blood, lest he that destroyed the firstborn should touch them. By faith they passed through the Red sea as by dry land: which the Egyptians assaying to do were drowned. By faith the walls of Jericho fell down, after they were compassed about seven days. By faith the harlot Rahab perished not with them that believed not, when she had received the spies with peace.

And what of Gedeon, and of Barak, and of Samson, and of Jephthae; of David also, and Samuel, and of the prophets: who through faith subdued kingdoms, wrought righteousness, obtained promises, stopped the mouths of lions. Quenched the violence of fire, escaped the edge of

the sword, out of weakness were made strong, waxed valiant in fight, turned to flight the armies of the aliens. Women received their dead raised to life again: and others were tortured, not accepting deliverance; that they might obtain a better resurrection: and others had trial of cruel mockings and scourgings, yea, moreover of bonds and imprisonment: they were stoned, they were sawn asunder, were tempted, were slain with the sword: they wandered about in sheepskins and goatskins; being destitute, afflicted, tormented; (Of whom the world was not worthy:) they wandered in deserts, and in mountains, and in dens and caves of the earth.

But the righteousness which is of faith speaketh on this wise say not in their heart, who shall ascend into heaven? (that is, to bring **Him** down from above:) or, who shall descend into the deep? (that is, to bring up **Him** again from the dead.) The word is nigh thee, even in thy mouth, and in thy heart: that is, the word of faith, wherefore **God** also hath highly exalted **Him**, and given **Him** a name which is above every name: that at **His** name every knee should bow, of things in heaven, and things in earth, and things under the earth.

Hence **He** drew forth the shade of the First Parent, and that of his son Abel, and of Noah, of Moses the lawgiver, and the obedient Abraham, patriarch, and Israel with his father and his children, and Rachel, for whose sake **He** did so much, and others many, and **He** made them blessed; and we must know, that earlier than these never were any human spirits saved. They bent their knee in **Him**, he is a new creature: old things are passed away; behold, all things are become new. ✚

Circle 2
"The Fields of Rape"

HUS **HE** DESCENDED OUT OF the first circle down to the second, that less space begirds, and so much greater dole, that goads to wailing. There standeth Minos horribly, and snarls; examines the transgressions at the entrance; judges, and sends according as he girds him. It is said that when the spirit evil-born cometh before him, wholly it confesses; and this discriminator of transgression seeth what place in Hell is meet for it; girds himself with his tail as many times as grades he wishes it should be thrust down. Always before him many of them stand; they go by turns each one unto the judgment; they speak, and hear, and then are downward hurled. "O! thou, that to this dolorous hostelry comest," said Minos to **Him**, when he saw **Him**, leaving the practice of so great an office, "There is therefore now no condemnation to them which are with **Thee**, who walk

not after the flesh, but after the Spirit. For the law of the Spirit of life in Thee hath made them free from the law of sin and death. For what the law could not do, in that it was weak through the flesh, God sending His own Son in the likeness of sinful flesh, and for sin, condemned sin in the flesh: that the righteousness of the law might be fulfilled in us, who walk not after the flesh, but after the Spirit. For they that are after the flesh do mind the things of the flesh; but they that are after the Spirit the things of the Spirit. For to be carnally minded is death; but to be spiritually minded is life and peace. Because the carnal mind is enmity against God: for it is not subject to the Law of God, neither indeed can be.

"And if Thee be in them, the body is dead because of sin; but the Spirit is life because of righteousness. But if the Spirit of Him that raised Thee up from the dead dwell in them, He that raised Thee up from the dead shall also quicken your mortal bodies by Thy Spirit that dwelleth in them. Therefore, they are debtors, not to the flesh, to live after the flesh. For if they live after the flesh, they shall die: but if they through the Spirit do mortify the deeds of the body, they shall live. For as many as are led by the Spirit of God, they are the sons of God. For they have not received the Spirit of bondage again to fear; but they have received the Spirit of adoption, whereby they cry, Abba, Father. The Spirit itself beareth witness with their spirit, that they are the children of God: and if children, then heirs; heirs of God, and joint-heirs with Thee; if so be that they suffer with Thee, that they may be also glorified together."

And he looked upon the mute companion and saith, "Thee I must gird myself with my tail as many times as grades thou must be thrust down condemned for thy crimes are—" and He held up his hand and staid his tail and Minos

acquiesced, allowing **Him** and **His** mute companion to pass unjudged and uncondemned.

And now began the dolesome notes to grow audible unto **Him**; now when **He** cometh there were much lamentation strikes upon **Him**. **He** came into a place mute of all light, which bellows as the sea does in a tempest, if by opposing winds it is combated. The infernal hurricane that never rests hurtles the spirits onward in its rapine; whirling them round, and smiting, it molests them.

When they arrived before the ruined precipice, ruined when the earth did quake and the rocks did rent and the veil of the temple was rent in twain from the top to the bottom upon the utterance of **His** cry upon the cross when **He** yielded up the ghost and the graves were opened; and many bodies of the dead which slept arose, and came out of the graves through the gaping maw rent in the walls of Asphodel Meadows and the Upper circles of Hades, and the lamenting dead entered into the holy city from the fires of faeces and of urine and of waste and of rubbish burned in the valley of Gehenna, where once the **LORD** saith to Jermiah the Prophet:

"O! kings of Judah, and inhabitants of Jerusalem; Behold, I will bring evil upon this place, the which whosoever heareth, his ears shall tingle. Because they have forsaken Me, and have estranged this place, and have burned incense in it unto other gods, whom neither they nor their fathers have known, nor the kings of Judah, and have filled this place with the blood of innocents; They have built also the high places of Baal, to burn their sons with fire for burnt offerings unto Baal, which I commanded not, nor spake it, neither came it into My mind: Therefore, behold, the days come, that this place shall no more be called Tophet, nor The Valley of the Son

of Hinnom, but The Valley of Slaughter." Only then at the behest and at the fiery sword were the dead returned by Gabriel and Michael and the hosts of Heaven, whom used mortar mixed with manna and stone to seal the breaches.

So when **He** and **His** Mute companion arrived before the ruined precipice, there are the shrieks, the plaints, and the laments, there they blaspheme the puissance divine. **He** understood that unto such a torment the carnal malefactors were condemned, who reason subjugate to appetite. And as the wings of starlings bear them on in the cold season in large band and full, so doth that blast the spirits maledict; it hither, thither, downward, upward, drives them; no hope doth comfort them for evermore, not of repose, but even of lesser pain. And as the cranes go chanting forth their lays, making in air a long line of themselves, so **He** saw coming, uttering lamentations, a woman whom he recognized for **He** knoweth beginning with Moses and with all the prophets, all things concerning the Scriptures. And the woman saith:

"When it came to pass in an eveningtide, that David the king from the depths of sleepless slumber did lumber upon the terrace of the palace perchance to sleep, perchance to warily weep, perchance his lusts reap, and then he saw me from his room, a woman quite aloof, washing myself on a neighbouring veranda. And by messenger sent in a letter did he entreat me with sweet words to retreat into his royal suite. He sought to seduce me, Bath-sheba, the wife of the Hittite, with prayers offered unto my moist folds most tight. But a fear of the **LORD God of Israel**, whose Commandments are nary trivial and couldst cost him an untimely burial. But my own prayers to my own gods were quite at odds with king awed with my bawd. And I sought to seduce David king with the singing of a song sung:

Thy intent to rape? Nay, faith! My consent
Giveth thee: thy ring signals thee a king.
Please, my aquiecence nary willsome.
Shalt the Lord God damn his King for spilt seed?
Pour thy milk-wine in my vase to come.
I plead, concede. David King relieveth needs.

"And I rent the clothes of David king whom was hesitant despite my consent and I bent to take in his musky scent. And with a complaintent Psalm doth David king protest:

Marry come up! I lean nayward. Fie! on
Thee, woman! Shalt I enwomb a scion
In thee in adultery? Thy husband,
The Hittite, fights tonight! A righteous man
Is Uriah in the eyes of our Lord.
His sword bloody with the gore of the horde.
Taketh thy leave. I shalt releave my needs;
Gasping fish upon the banks art my seed.

"And I mistook not his intent not, so I took without the king's consent, reading from the Book of Pornè were we decadent in a hidden nook, our discontent ended from our lusts rent:

From Hell escape thee! Then David rape me!
Eat me, beat me, mistreat me! Discreet us
Upon this roof be. Behoof quietus
Cometh quickly, runneth sickly thy sperm-
Vomited in my basin from thy worm.

"And in accordance with the Laws of the LORD God

The lustful Rape of Bath-sheba by David the King!

of Israel, having had his seed of copulation gone out from him and thus into me, then David King was unclean and washed all his flesh in water and I, the woman, with whom David King lied with the seed of copulation, did we both bathe ourselves. The heat of the water in the pool reignited the flames of flirtation and an addition of seed of copulation issued from his loins into mine. We found ourselves clean and again unclean and clean and again unclean until the morningtide."

And He rebuked Bath-sheba and said unto her, **"Have ye not read, O! Queen of Jerusalem, that He which made them at the beginning made them male and female, and said, 'For this cause shall a man leave father and mother, and shall cleave to his wife: and they twain shall be one flesh? Wherefore they are no more twain, but one flesh.' What therefore God hath joined together, let not man put asunder."**

"Divorce?" Bath-sheba said laughing, "Of that sin I have no remorse nor liveth in its shadow, because a widow I am. On the field of battle did my husband die. Rattled by Uriah's death I was, and prattled nonsense like a babe, but David king and Solomon whom was growing within my womb, comforted me when in a tomb I buried my husband."

And hailstones were cast down from suddenly formed thunderous storm clouds and buffeted Bath-sheba bruising her breast, blackening her eyes, and she shrieked in cries of wailing for this was a new anguish, a new agony. He who is without sin; for He hath made Him to be sin for us, who knew no sin; that we might be made the righteousness of God in Him; since we have not an high priest which cannot be touched with the feeling of our infirmities; but was in all points tempted like as we are, yet without sin; forasmuch as we know that we were not redeemed with corruptible

things, as silver and gold, from your vain conversation received by tradition from our fathers, but with the precious blood of **Christ**, as of a lamb without blemish and without spot, so **He** cast the first hail stone.

There is therefore now no condemnation to them which are in **Him**, who walk not after the flesh, but after the **Spirit**. For the Law of the **Spirit** of life in **Him** hath made us free from the Law of sin and death. For what the Law could not do, in that it was weak through the flesh, **God** sending **His** own **Son** in the likeness of sinful flesh, and for sin, condemned sin in the flesh: that the righteousness of the Law might be fulfilled in us, who walk not after the flesh, but after the **Spirit**. For they that are after the flesh do mind the things of the flesh; but they that are after the **Spirit** the things of the **Spirit**. For to be carnally minded is death; but to be spiritually minded is life and peace. Because the carnal mind is enmity against **God**: for it is not subject to the Law of **God**, neither indeed can be. So then they that are in the flesh cannot please **God**. But ye are not in the flesh, but in the **Spirit**, if so be that the **Spirit** of **God** dwell in you. Now if any man have not the **Spirit** of **Christ**, he is none of his. And if **He** be in us, the body is dead because of sin; but the **Spirit** is life because of righteousness. But if the **Spirit** of **Him** that raised up **His Son** from the dead dwell in us, **He** that raised up **His Son** from the dead shall also quicken your mortal bodies by his **Spirit** that dwelleth in us.

Then **His** mute companion saw in and pointed into the distance, clouds hanging under the roof of the cave as if the smoke of a furnace and balls of fire and brimstone out of heaven rained down onto a small sea to the south, which being fed by the trickling stream from the tempest to the north. The rain of brimstone and fire set the sea alight

and the surface burned in an unending blaze. As He and His mute companion compassed safely around the heat and glow of the conflagration, they encountered along the shore of the searing sea a pillar of salt in the shape of a woman.

And in a nearby cave, two woman, Miriam and Paltith, and their father, Lot, whom slumbered into eternity as though drunk on wine. And He heard the echoes on the whispering winds of their plots that the firstborn once saith unto the younger, "Our father is old, and there is not a man in the earth to come in unto us after the manner of all the earth: come, let us make our father drink wine, and we will lie with him, that we may preserve seed of our father," and again "Behold, I lay yesternight with my father: let us make him drink wine this night also; and go thou in, and lie with him, that we may preserve seed of our father."

He beheld the daughters of Lot, as they travailed in the multiplicity of their sorrow and their conception, in pain they brought forth fat stones as if children, which turned to succulent bread and they consumed said bread for they were hungered, and again conceived and the stone grew in the comfort of their womb and they travailed in the multiplicity of their sorrow and their conception, in pain they brought forth fat stones as if children which turned to succulent bread and they consumed said bread for they were hungered, and again conceived and the stone grew in the comfort of their womb and they travailed in the multiplicity of their sorrow and their conception, in pain they brought forth fat stones as if children.

"Thy father, Lot," He saith unto them, "who not only kept himself sober and chaste in Sodom, but was a constant mourner for the wickedness of the place and a

The lustful Rape of Lot by his daughters after the destruction of Sodom!

witness against it, was yet, in the mountain, where he was alone, and as he thought quite out of the way of temptation, shamefully overtaken. Let him therefore that thinks he stands, stands high and stands firm, take heed lest he fall. No mountain, on this side the holy hill above, can set us out of the reach of Satan's fiery darts. A man may do that without reluctance, when he is drunk, which, when he is sober, he could not think of without horror. Even from our dearest relations and friends, whom we love, and esteem, and expect kindness from. Lot, whose temperance and chastity were impregnable against the batteries of foreign force, was surprised into sin and shame by the base treachery of his own daughters: we must dread a snare wherever we are, and be always upon our guard. No excuse can be made for the daughters, nor for Lot. Scarcely any account can be given of the affair but this: the heart is deceitful above all things, and desperately wicked: who can know it?[1]"

And Miriam, the firstborn of Lot protested, notwithstanding travailing in the perpetual birthing of the stone, "My child and my nephew, Moab and Ben-Ammi, the fathers of two great nations, neighbours to Israel, and Assur also is joined with them: they have holpen the children of Lot," she paused to push in her anguish, "Though prosperous births may attend incestuous conceptions, yet they are so far from justifying them that they rather perpetuate the reproach of them and entail infamy upon posterity; yet the tribe of Judah, of which our **Lord** sprang, descended from such a birth, and Ruth, a Moabitess, has a name in **Thy** own genealogy: for we know whom **Thee** are, Christ. **I am Thy mother!**" and **He** said, as **He** and **His** mute companion retreated out of the cave by the way of a path in the side of the mountain, "Get thee behind Me, Satan." ✝

---

1 Henry, Matthew, *Commentary on the Whole Bible*, abridged

Circle 3
"Gorging on the Fruit of Good and Evil"

T THE RETURN OF CON-sciousness, that closed before the pity of those two relations, which utterly with sadness had confused **His** companion, new torments he beholds, and new tormented around him, whichsoever way he moves, and whichsoever way he turns, and gazes. In the third circle is he of the rain eternal, maledict, and cold, and heavy; its law and quality are never new. Huge hail, and water sombre-hued, and snow, athwart the tenebrous air pour down amain; noisome the earth is, that receiveth this.

Cerberus, monster cruel and uncouth, with his three gullets like a dog barked over the people that are there submerged. Red eyes he has, and unctuous beard and black, and belly large, and armed with claws his hands; he rends the spirits, flays, and quarters them. Howl the rain maketh them like unto dogs; one side they make a shelter for the

other; oft turn themselves the wretched reprobates. When Cerberus perceived them, the great worm! His mouths he opened, and displayed his tusks; not a limb had he that was motionless.

And **He**, the **Merciful Conductor**, with **His** spans extended, took of the earth, and with **His** fists well filled, **He** threw it into those rapacious gullets. Such as that dog is, who by barking craves, and quiet grows soon as his food he gnaws, for to devour it he but thinks and struggles, the like became those muzzles filth-begrimed of Cerberus the demon, who so thunders over the souls that they would fain be deaf.

They passed across the shadows, which subdues the heavy rain-storm, and they placed their feet upon their vanity that person seems. They all were lying prone upon the earth, excepting one, who sat upright as soon as she beheld them passing on before her. "O! **Thou** that conducts **Thyself** through this Hell," the woman said to **Him**, "recall me, if thou canst **Thyself** wast made before I was unmade."

"**Did not the serpent say unto the thee, woman, 'Yea, hath God said, "Ye shall not eat of every tree of the garden"?' Were ye not allowed to eat of the fruit of the trees of the garden: but of the fruit of the tree which is in the midst of the garden, God hath said, 'Ye shall not eat of it, neither shall ye touch it, lest ye die'? And did not the serpent tempt, 'Ye shall not surely die: for God doth know that in the day ye eat thereof, then your eyes shall be opened, and ye shall be as gods, knowing good and evil'? Did ye now see that the tree was good for food, and that it was pleasant to the eyes, and a tree to be desired to make one wise, thee took of the fruit thereof, and did eat, and gave also unto thy husband with thee; and he**

Eve is gluttonous for the fruit of the tree of the knowledge of Good and Evil!

did eat; and the eyes of ye both were opened, and ye knew that ye were naked; and ye sewed fig leaves together, and made themselves aprons? Ye did.

"Were ye not a glutton to desire to eat of the fruit of the tree of the knowledge of both good and evil? And a drunkard on the wine of the indulgence in the revelry of this knowledge?"

And the woman protested, "I knew not the knowledge that the LORD God would greatly multiply my sorrow and my conception; in sorrow I brought forth children; and my desire wouldst be to my husband, and he shall rule over me! I knew not that when my husband hearkened unto my voice, cursed would be the ground for his sake; in sorrow shalt he eat of it all the days of his life; thorns also and thistles shall it bring forth to he; and he shalt eat the herb of the field; in the sweat of his face shalt he eat bread, till he return unto the ground; for out of it wast he taken: for dust he art, and unto dust shalt he return! I knew not that the LORD God would sent us forth from the garden of Eden, to till the ground from whence he was taken.

"If I had known the knowledge that the serpent, because he hast done this, cursed above all cattle, and above every beast of the field; upon his belly shalt he go, and dust shalt he eat all the days of his life: I would have done it time and time again if the chance I could, because of me along hath the LORD God, Thy Father, hath put enmity between him and me, and between his seed and my seed, whom art Thee; Thee hath bruised his head, and he hath bruised Thy heel."

"Because of thee alone, thy children in the first days when the earth was corrupt and filled with violence through them and those in the of last days perilous times shall come. For men were, are, and shall be lovers

of their own selves, covetous, boasters, proud, blasphemers, disobedient to parents, unthankful, unholy, without natural affection, trucebreakers, false accusers, incontinent, fierce, despisers of those that are good,traitors, heady, highminded, lovers of pleasures more than lovers of God; having a form of godliness, but denying the power thereof: from such turn away. For of this sort are they which creep into houses, and lead captive silly women laden with sins, led away with divers lusts, ever learning, and instead always seeking the knowledge of good and evil and never able to come to the knowledge of the Truth."

"Because of me, alone, art Thou come down from heaven, not to do Thy own will, but the will of Him that sent Thee," the woman bragged, "The LORD God hath set forth to be a propitiation through faith in Thy blood, to declare Thy righteousness for the remission of sins that are past, through the forbearance of God; to declare, I say, at this time Thy righteousness: that Thee might be just, and the justifier of him which believeth in Thee. For then must Thee often have suffered since the foundation of the world: but now once in the end of the world hath Thee appeared to put away sin by the sacrifice of Thyself. Thee came as a light into the world, that whosoever believeth on Thee should not abide in darkness. To this end was Thee born, and for this cause came Thee into the world, that Thee should bear witness unto the truth. Every one that is of the truth heareth Thy voice.

"It was because of me that the serpent sinneth from the beginning. For this purpose was Thee manifested, that Thee might destroy the works of the devil. The fruit of the tree of the knowledge of good and evil was uprooted so that Thee can be the living bread which came down from heav-

en: if any man eat of this bread, he shall live for ever: and the bread that **Thee** will give is **Thy** flesh, which **Thee** will give for the life of the world.

"Because of me art **Thou**, who being in the form of **God**, thought it not robbery to be equal with **God**: but made **Thyself** of no reputation, and took upon **Thou** the form of a servant, and was made in the likeness of men: and being found in fashion as a **Man**, **Thee** humbled **Thyself**, and became obedient unto death, even the death of the cross.

"Nevertheless death reigned from my husband Adam to Moses, even over them that had not sinned after the similitude of Adam's transgression, who is the figure of him that was to come. But not as the offence, so also is the free gift. For if through the offence of one many be dead, much more the grace of the **LORD God**, and the gift by grace, which is by one man, **Thee** hath abounded unto many.

"Because of me alone art **Thou** their peace, who hath made both one, and hath broken down the middle wall of partition between my children; having abolished in **Thy** flesh the enmity, even the law of commandments contained in ordinances; for to make in **Thyself** of twain one new man, so making peace; and that **Thy** might reconcile both unto God in one body by the cross, having slain the enmity thereby: and came and preached peace to my children which were afar off, and to them that were nigh. For through **Thee** their both have access by one **Spirit** unto the **Father**.

"Because of me alone, was the earth corrupt and filled with violence and the **LORD God** so loved the world, that **He** gave **His** only begotten **Son**, that whosoever believeth in **Thee** should not perish, but have everlasting life. For the **LORD God** sent not **His Son** into the world to condemn the world; but that the world through **Thee** might be saved.

He that believeth on **Thee** is not condemned: but he that believeth not is condemned already, because he hath not believed in the name of the only begotten **Son of God**. And it is because I ate the fruit of the tree of the knowledge of good and evil that this condemnation happened, that light is come into the world, and men loved darkness rather than light, because their deeds were evil. It is becasue every one that doeth evil hateth the light, neither cometh to the light, lest his deeds should be reprove; but he that doeth truth cometh to the light, that his deeds may be made manifest, that they are wrought in the **LORD God**!

"**Because of me alone art Thou! Because of me alone!**"

Circle 4
"Amorous Avarice of the Husbandman"

PAPE SATAN, PAPE SATAN, Aleppe!" Thus Plutus with his clucking voice began; and **He**, who all things knew, said, to encourage **His** mute companion: **"Let not thy fear harm thee; for any power that he may have shall not prevent thy going down this crag."** Then **He** turned round unto that bloated lip, and said: **"Be silent, thou accursed wolf; consume within thyself with thine own rage. Not causeless is this journey to the abyss; thus is it willed on high, where Michael wrought vengeance upon the proud adultery."**

Thus they descended into the fourth chasm, gaining still farther on the dolesome shore which all the woe of the universe insacks. Justice of **God**, ah! who heaps up so many new toils and sufferings as they beheld? and why doth our transgression waste us so? As doth the billow there upon

Charybdis, that breaks itself on that which it encoun-
ters, so here the folk must dance their roundelay.

Here saw they people, more than elsewhere, many,
on one side and the other, with great howls, rolling
weights forward by main force of chest. They clashed together, and then at that point each one turned backward,
rolling retrograde, crying, "Why keepest?" and, "Why
squanderest thou?" Thus they returned along the lurid circle on either hand unto the opposite point, shouting their
shameful metre evermore.

Then each, when **His** mute companion arrived there,
wheeled about through his half-circle to another joust; and
His mute companion was astonished when he encountered
a character from one of **His** parables, always under the as-
sumption that these were fairy stories set to inspire faith, but
nay faith! the mute companion saw a husbandman being
tormented in Hades. And the husbandman exclaimed unto
his fellow husbandmen, "My Master, a certain householder,
which planted a vineyard, and hedged it round about, and
digged a winepress in it, and built a tower, and let it out to
husbandmen, and went into a far country: and when the
time of the fruit drew near, he sent his servants to the us,
that they might receive the fruits of it. And we took his servants, and beat one, and killed another, and stoned another.
Again, he sent other servants more than the first: and they
did unto them likewise. But last of all he sent unto us his
son, saying, 'They will reverence my son.' But when we saw
the son, we said among themselves, 'This is the heir; come,
let us kill him, and let us seize on his inheritance.' And we
caught him, and cast him out of the vineyard, and slew him.
When the lord therefore of the vineyard cometh, he miserably destroyed those us wicked men, and let out his vineyard
unto other husbandmen, which shall render him the fruits

in their seasons."

And **He** had saith unto the husbandman as he had unto **His** Disciples, **"Did ye never read in the scriptures, 'The stone which the builders rejected, the same is become the head of the corner: this is the Lord's doing, and it is marvellous in our eyes?' Therefore say I unto you, The kingdom of God shall be taken from you, and given to a nation bringing forth the fruits thereof. And whosoever shall fall on this stone shall be broken: but on whomsoever it shall fall, it will grind him to powder."**

They crossed the circle to the other bank, near to a fount that boils, and pours itself along a gully that runs out of it. The water was more sombre far than perse; and they, in company with the dusky waves, made entrance downward by a path uncouth. A marsh it maked, which has the name of Styx, this tristful brooklet, when it has descended down to the foot of the malign gray shores.

And **His** mute companion, who stood intent upon beholding, saw people mud-besprent in that lagoon, all of them naked and with angry look. They smote each other not alone with hands, but with the head and with the breast and feet, tearing each other piecemeal with their teeth. And a passerby on his own journey saith to the mute companion: "Son, thou now beholdest the souls of those whom anger overcame; and likewise I would have thee know for certain beneath the water people are who sigh and make this water bubble at the surface, as the eye tells thee wheresoe'er it turns. Fixed in the mire they say, 'We sullen were in the sweet air, which by the sun is gladdened, bearing within ourselves the sluggish reek; now we are sullen in this sable mire.' This hymn do they keep gurgling in their throats, for

The greedful husbandmen slay the servants and son of the vineyard!

with unbroken words they cannot say it."

Thus the two went circling round the filthy fen a great arc 'twixt the dry bank and the swamp, with eyes turned unto those who gorge the mire; unto the foot of a tower they came at last. ✠

Circle 5
"The Froth of the Wroth of Herod"

HAT LONG BEFORE THEY TO the foot of that high tower had come, their eyes went upward to the summit of it, by reason of two flamelets they saw placed there, and from afar another answer them, so far, that hardly could the eye attain it.

Cord never shot an arrow from itself that sped away athwart the air so swift, as I beheld a very little boat come over the water towords us at that moment, under the guidance of a single pilot, who shouted, "Now art thou arrived, fell soul?"

"Phlegyas, Phlegyas, thou criest out in vain for this once," He said; "Thou shalt not have us longer than in the passing of the slough." As he who listens to some great deceit that has been done to him, and then resents it, such became Phlegyas, in his gathered wrath.

45

He and **His** mute companion descended down into the boat, the antique prow went on its way, dividing more of the water than 'tis wont with others. While they were running through the dead canal, uprose in front of them one full of mire, and said, "How art **Thou** a man? How didst **Thou** live through the massacre in Bethlehem? I was the one mocked of the wise men, and exceeding wroth, and sent forth, and slew all the children that were in Bethlehem, and in all the coasts thereof, from two years old and under, according to the time which he had diligently inquired of the wise men. Who art **Thou** that comest ere the hour?" And **He** to him: **"Although I come, I stay not; but who art thou that hast become so squalid?"** "**Thou** seest that I am one who weeps," he answered. And **He** to him: **"With weeping and with wailing, thou spirit maledict, do thou remain; for thee I know, though thou art all defiled."**

Then stretched he both his hands unto the boat; whereat the mute and wary companion thrust him back, as if to say, "Away there with the other dogs!" Thereafter with his arms he clasped **His** neck; he kissed **His** face, and as if to say, "Disdainful soul, blessed be she who bore thee in her bosom. That was an arrogant person in the world goodness is none, that decks his memory; so likewise here his shade is furious. How many are esteemed great kings up there, who here shall be like unto swine in mire, leaving behind them horrible dispraises!" A little after that, **He** saw such havoc made of Herod by the people of the mire, that **He** praised and thank **His God** for it.

A little after that, **His** mute companion saw such havoc made of Herod by the people of the mire, that still the mute silently praised and thanked his **God** for it. The

---

The wrothful pluck Herod back into the muck and mire of the river Styx!

damned stuck in the muck grasped and clawed at Herod pulling him from his grasp on the ship and into their own grasp, rasping and gnashing their teeth at the whom dared massacre the innocents of Bethlehem and dared desert the slog of bog of the river of the Styx. Herod shrieked at his bleak fate, howling and wailing to free himself from the torments of his wrath against the poor and innocent babes of Bethlehem, whom grew not, whom married not, whom bore children not. Such was the destiny of a king of Jews who sought to halt the merciless advance of prophecy by searching for the infant **Christ**, not to fall down, and worship **Him** nor open his treasures he should then present unto **Him** gifts of gold and frankincense and myrrh, but rather being exceeding wroth, and sending forth men, and slaying all the children that were in Bethlehem, and in all the coasts thereof, from two years old and under, according to the time which he had diligently inquired of the wise men.

They left Herod there, and more of him their is nothing to tell; but on **His** ears there smote a lamentation, whence forward **He** intent unbars **His** eyes. Even now, the city draweth near whose name is Dis, with the grave citizens, with the great throng. Its mosques already, clearly within there in the valley **His** mute companion discerned vermilion, as if issuing from the fire. The fire eternal that kindles them within makes them look red, as he beholdest in this nether Hell.

Then they arrived within the moats profound, that circumvallate that disconsolate city; the walls appeared to him to be of iron. Not without making first a circuit wide, they came unto a place where loud the pilot cried out to us, "Debark, here is the entrance."

More than a thousand at the gates they saw out of the

Heavens rained down, who angrily were saying, "Who is this that conquered death and walketh through the kingdom of the people dead? Why doth **Thee** descend into Hell, instead of descending from heaven with a shout, with the voice of the archangel, and with the trump of God: and only then shalt the dead in **Thee** shall rise first? How are the we, the dead, raised up? and with what body doth we come?"

And **He** answereth the dead of thousands, **"Thou fools, that which thou sowest is not quickened, except it die: and that which thou sowest, thou sowest not that body that shall be, but bare grain, it may chance of wheat, or of some other grain: but God giveth it a body as it hath pleased Him, and to every seed His own body. All flesh is not the same flesh: but there is one kind of flesh of men, another flesh of beasts, another of fishes, and another of birds. There are also celestial bodies, and bodies terrestrial: but the glory of the celestial is one, and the glory of the terrestrial is another. There is one glory of the sun, and another glory of the moon, and another glory of the stars: for one star differeth from another star in glory.**

"So also is the resurrection of the dead. It is sown in corruption; it is raised in incorruption: it is sown in dishonour; it is raised in glory: it is sown in weakness; it is raised in power: it is sown a natural body; it is raised a spiritual body.

"There is a natural body, and there is a spiritual body. And so it is written, the first man Adam was made a living soul; the last Adam was made a quickening spirit. Howbeit that was not first which is spiritual, but that which is natural; and afterward that which is spiritual. The first man is of the earth, earthy; the second man is the Lord from heaven. As is the earthy, such are they also

that are earthy: and as is the heavenly, such are they also that are heavenly. And as we have borne the image of the earthy, we shall also bear the image of the heavenly.

"Now this I say, brethren, that flesh and blood cannot inherit the kingdom of God; neither doth corruption inherit incorruption. Behold! I shew you a mystery; some shall not all sleep, but we shall all be changed, in a moment, in the twinkling of an eye, at the last trump: for the trumpet shall sound, and the dead shall be raised incorruptible, and some shall be changed. For this corruptible must put on incorruption, and this mortal must put on immortality. So when this corruptible shall have put on incorruption, and this mortal shall have put on immortality, then shall be brought to pass the saying that is written, Death is swallowed up in victory. O! death, where is thy sting? O! grave, where is thy victory? The sting of death is sin; and the strength of sin is the law."

And the dead each within in rivalry ran back and they closed the portals. And **He** sat upon a rock and the great patience waited. Beyond the walls, the dead taunted **Him** with mock worship. More than a thousand ruined souls the mute saw, thus fleeing from before one who on foot was passing o'er the Styx with soles unwet. From off his face he fanned that unctuous air, waving his left hand oft in front of him, and only with that anguish seemed he weary. Hundreds sent from Heaven were they, and to **Him** one turned and saith unto the dead, "O! banished out of **heaven**, people despised! Whence is this arrogance within you couched? wherefore recalcitrate against that will, from which the end can never be cut off, and which has many times increased your pain? What helpeth it to butt against the fates? Your

Cerberus, if you remember well, for that still bears his chin and gullet peeled."

Then **He** staid his hand and saith unto the angels of the **LORD**, **"See, I have given into thine hand Dis, and the king thereof, and the thousands of ruined souls within. And ye shall compass the city, all ye men of war, and go round about the city once. Thus shalt thou do six days. And seven angels shall bear before the ark seven trumps of thy trumpets: and the seventh day ye shall compass the city seven times, and the angel shall blow with the trumpets. And it shall come to pass, that when ye make a long blast with thy trumpets, and when ye hear the sound of the trumpet, all the angel shall shout with a great shout; and the wall of the city shall fall down flat."**

And it came to pass that the angels of the **LORD** did as instructed and the walls of the city of Dis rumbled then crumbled then fell down flat. And the dead cried out in sudden shock for they hath endlessly endured symbolic suffering and poetic pain and theatrical tortures and allegorical agnoies in Hades for their sins in their lives before and wouldst very well know further misfortune knowing that **His** words to them as **He** passed through the ruins shalt come to pass that: **"Cursed be the man before the Lord, that riseth up and buildeth this city Dis."** ✝

Circle6
"The Briefest Hiatus with the Heretics"

**HE MUTE WHOSE INCLINA-**tion had to see what the condition such a fortress holds, soon as he was within, cast round his eye, and see on every hand an ample plain, full of distress and torment terrible. The sepulchres make all the place uneven; so likewise did they there on every side, saving that there the manner was more bitter; for flames between the sepulchres were scattered, by which they so intensely heated were, that iron more so asks not any art. All of their coverings uplifted were, and from them issued forth such dire laments, sooth seemed they of the wretched and tormented.

Upon the margin of a lofty bank which great rocks broken in a circle made, they came upon a still more cruel throng; and there, by reason of the horrible excess of stench the deep abyss throws out, they drew ourselves aside behind

the cover of a great tomb, whereon the Mute saw a writing, which said in a language he spoke not. And a Roman, a poet named Virgil, found **Him** and **His** Mute companion sitting on some rocks and reading the inscription of the tomb, Virgil, ferrying his own chronologically displaced companion on a journey that paralleled the pilgrimage **He** and **His** Mute companion were on and therefore warned **Him** of what awaited them beyond the circle numbered sixth:

"Upon the inside of these rocks," began he then to say, "are three small circles, from grade to grade, like those which thou art leaving. They all are full of spirits maledict; but that hereafter sight alone suffice thee, hear how and wherefore they are in constraint. Of every malice that wins hate in Heaven, injury is the end; and all such end either by force or fraud afflicteth others. But because fraud is man's peculiar vice, more it displeases **God**; and so stand lowest the fraudulent, and greater dole assails them.

"All the first circle of the Violent is; but since force may be used against three persons, in three rounds 'tis divided and constructed. To **God**, to ourselves, and to our neighbour can we use force; I say on them and on their things, as thou shalt hear with reason manifest.

"A death by violence, and painful wounds, are to our neighbour given; and in his substance ruin, and arson, and injurious levies; whence homicides, and he who smites unjustly, marauders, and freebooters, the first round tormenteth all in companies diverse. Man may lay violent hands upon himself and his own goods; and therefore in the second round must perforce without avail repent whoever of your world deprives himself, who games, and dissipates his property, and weepeth there, where he should jocund be. Violence can be done the **Deity**, in heart denying and blas-

pheming Him and Thee, and by disdaining Nature and her bounty. And for this reason doth the smallest round seal with its signet Sodom and Cahors, and who, disdaining God, speaks from the heart. Fraud, wherewithal is every conscience stung, a man may practise upon him who trusts, and him who doth no confidence imburse.

"This latter mode, it would appear, dissevers only the bond of love which Nature makes; wherefore within the second circle nestle hypocrisy, flattery, and who deals in magic, falsification, theft, and simony, panders, and barrators, and the like filth. By the other mode, forgotten is that love which Nature makes, and what is after added, from which there is a special faith engendered.

"Hence in the smallest circle, where the point is of the Universe, upon which Dis is seated, whoever betrays for ever is consumed."

And Virgil, proud of his pompous, yet pedantic poetry, howbeit only then realized he was speaking to the Architect of Solomon's Temple Whom had ordered through an angel of the LORD the house of the LORD built at Jerusalem in mount Moriah, where the LORD appeared unto David his father, in the place that David had prepared in the threshingfloor of Ornan the Jebusite. He also and alone was the Architect of all of nine circles of the Inferno and the designer of all of the apt agony and poetic punishments found within and required no assistance nor map to traverse its depths. Virgil bowed to Him in feigned, or perchance forced, genuflection and allowed Him and His Mute companion to pass free of further assault of by poet. ✠

Virgil, ferrying his own chronologically displaced companion Dante Alighieri passed two souls entwined in combat, paused to instruct Him *in the architecture of the Inferno, not realizing* He *is the Architect!*

Circle 7 – Ring 1
"The Roiling, Boiling River of Blood"

HE PLACE WHERE TO DE-scend the bank we came was alpine, and from what was there, moreover, of such a kind that every eye would shun it. Such as that ruin is which in the flank smote, either by earthquake or by failing stay, for from the mountain's top, from which it moved, unto the plain the cliff is shattered so, some path 'twould give to him who was above. Even such was the descent of that ravine, and on the border of the broken chasm the infamy of Jericho was stretched along, who was conceived in the fictitious cow; and when he us beheld, he bit himself, even as one whom anger racks within.

He towards him shouted: "Peradventure thou think'st that here may be the Procurator of Rome, who in the world above brought death to thee? Get thee gone, beast, for this one cometh not instructed by thy sister, but he

56

comes in order to behold your punishments."

As is that bull who breaks loose at the moment in which he has received the mortal blow, who cannot walk, but staggers here and there, the Minotaur beheld the mute do the like; and he, the wary, cried: "Run to the passage; while he wroth, 'tis well thou shouldst descend."

Thus down they took they way o'er that discharge of stones, which oftentimes did move themselves beneath His feet, from the unwonted burden. Thoughtful He went; and He said: **"Thou art thinking perhaps upon this ruin, which is guarded by that brute anger which just now I quenched. Now will I have thee know, the other time I was here as Architect and builder of the nether Hell, this precipice had not yet fallen down. But truly, if I well discern, a little before My coming who the mighty spoil bore off from Dis, in the supernal circle, upon all sides the deep and loathsome valley trembled upon My death so, that I thought the Universe was thrilled with love, by which there are who think the world ofttimes converted into chaos; and at that moment this primeval crag both here and elsewhere made such overthrow. But fix thine eyes below; for draweth near the river of blood, within which boiling is whoe'er by violence doth injure others."**

The mute thought, "O! blind cupidity, O! wrath insane, that spurs us onward so in our short life, and in the eternal then so badly steeps us!" He saw an ample moat bent like a bow, as one which all the plain encompasses, conformable to what his **Guide** had said. And between this and the embankment's foot Centaurs in file were running, armed with arrows, as in the world they used the chase to follow. Beholding them descend, each one stood still, and from the squadron three detached themselves, with bows and arrows in advance selected; and from afar one cried: "Unto what

torment come ye, who down the hillside are descending? Tell us from there; if not, I draw the bow."

He said: "Our answer will we make to Chiron, near you there; in evil hour, that will of thine was evermore so hasty." Then He touched the mute, and said: "This one is Nessus, who perished for the lovely Dejanira, and for himself, himself did vengeance take. And he in the midst, who at his breast is gazing, is the great Chiron, who brought up Achilles; that other Pholus is, who was so wrathful. Thousands and thousands go about the moat shooting with shafts whatever soul emerges out of the blood, more than his crime allots."

Near they approached unto those monsters fleet; Chiron an arrow took, and with the notch backward upon his jaws he put his beard. After he had uncovered his great mouth, he said to the companions of his squadron: "Are you ware that he behind moveth whate'er He touches? Thus are not wont to do the feet of dead men. Yet He appears unto us as both of the living and of the dead. How can He be both living and dead?"

And the good Guide, who now was at his breast, where the two natures are together joined, replied: "Indeed I live, and thus alone Me it behoves to show him the dark valley; necessity, and not delight, impels us. Some one withdrew from singing Halleluja, who unto Me committed this new office; no thief am I, nor I a thievish spirit. But by that virtue through which I am moving My steps along this savage thoroughfare, give us some one of thine, to be with us, and who may show us where to pass the ford, and who may carry this one on his back; for 'tis no spirit that can walk the air."

Upon his right breast Chiron wheeled about, and said to Nessus: "Turn and do thou guide them, and warn aside,

if other band may meet you." They with their faithful escort onward moved along the brink of the vermilion boiling, wherein the boiled were uttering loud laments. People they saw within up to the eyebrows, and the great Centaur said: "Tyrants are these, who dealt in bloodshed and in pillaging. Here they lament their pitiless mischiefs; here is Alexander, and fierce Dionysius who upon Sicily brought dolorous years. That forehead there which has the hair so black is Azzolin; and the other who is blond, Obizzo is of Esti, who, in truth, up in the world was by his stepson slain."

A little farther on the Centaur stopped above a folk, who far down as the throat seemed from that boiling stream to issue forth. A shade he showed us on one side alone, saying: "He cleft asunder in God's bosom the heart that still upon the Thames is honoured." Then people saw **Him**, who from out the river lifted their heads and also all the chest; and many among these **He** recognised. Thus ever more and more grew shallower that blood, so that the feet alone it covered; and there across the moat our passage was. "Even as thou here upon this side beholdest the boiling stream, that aye diminishes," the Centaur said, "I wish thee to believe That on this other more and more declines its bed, until it reunites itself where it behoveth tyranny to groan. Justice divine, upon this side, is goading that Xerxes, who was a scourge on earth, and Pyrrhus, and Sextus; and for ever milks the tears which with the boiling it unseals—"

And one of the souls in the roiling, boiling river of blood reached the embankment and reached with out-stretched hand towards **Him**, and the centaurs readied their bows, drawing the bowstring to their beards and prepared to loose the bolts, when **He** stayed them with a raised hand. And the soul said, "The **LORD God of Israel** once, during

my life, saith, 'And when thy days be fulfilled, and thou shalt sleep with thy fathers, I will set up thy seed after thee, which shall proceed out of thy bowels, and I will establish his kingdom. He shall build an house for My name, and I will stablish the throne of His kingdom for ever. I will be His father, and He shall be My Son. If He commit iniquity, I will chasten Him with the rod of men, and with the stripes of the children of men: but my mercy shall not depart away from Him, as I took it from Saul, whom I put away before thee. And thine house and thy kingdom shall be established for ever before thee: thy throne shall be established for ever.' And I knoweth, although I know not how I know the knowledge that you are a descendent of my loins. For The Lord said unto Thee, 'Sit Thou at my right hand, until I make thine enemies Thy footstool.' The Lord sendeth the rod of Thy strength out of Zion: rule Thou in the midst of Thine enemies. Thy people shall be willing in the day of thy power, in the beauties of holiness from the womb of the morning: Thou hast the dew of Thy youth. The LORD hath sworn, and will not repent, 'Thou art a priest for ever after the order of Melchizedek.'

"I beholdeth, the days hath come, as did the LORD saith, that the LORD will raise unto me a righteous Branch, and a King shall reign and prosper, and shall execute judgment and justice in the earth. In Thy days Judah shall be saved, and Israel shall dwell safely: and this is The name whereby Thou shall be called, THE LORD OUR RIGHTEOUSNESS! Thus saith Thy father in Heaven, and thus as Thy father in Jerusalem, save me from the slings and arrows of these beasts that keepeth me in the roiling, boiling river of blood!"

And He saith unto David King, "But are ye come

unto mount Sion, and unto the city of the living God, the heavenly Jerusalem, and to an innumerable company of angels, to the general assembly and church of the firstborn, which are written in heaven, and to God the Judge of all, and to the spirits of just men made perfect, to Me the mediator of the new covenant, and to the blood of sprinkling, that speaketh better things than that of Abel? Or are ye a dweller upon the earth whom worship the Beast, whose name is not written in the book of life of the Lamb slain from the foundation of the world? There shall in no wise enter into it any thing that defileth, neither whatsoever worketh abomination, or maketh a lie: but they which are written in the Lamb's book of life."

"**But I am Thy father!**" David the king pleaded.

And appeared around **His** waist a pouch from which **He** pulled the book of life, that is also called the **Word of God**, and **He,** as **He** did in life, preached with authority in the synagogue and now read from the Books of Samuel. **He** posed questions onto David the king, though **He** sought not the answers for **He** was learned in the scriptures and knew all the answers to all of the questions:

"**Did thee not send for Uriah the Hittite?**" And David was silent. "**When Uriah was come unto thee, did thee not demand of him how the people did, and how the war prospered? Did thee not saith to Uriah, 'Go down to thy house, and wash thy feet.' So that Bath-sheba, commanded by thy orders, could rape her husband into receiving the milk of his stones and deceiving his servants into believing thy bastard is his legitimate scion, the heir to the Hittite's household. And when thy servants saw he went not down to his house, did thee not say, 'Camest thou not from thy journey? why then didst thou not go down**

unto thine house?' And faithful and good Uriah saith unto thee, 'The ark, and Israel, and Judah, abide in tents; and my lord Joab, and the servants of my lord, are encamped in the open fields; shall I then go into mine house, to eat and to drink, and to lie with my wife? as thou livest, and as thy soul liveth, I will not do this thing.' " And David remained silent. "And did thee not say unto Uriah, 'Tarry here to day also, and to morrow I will let thee depart'? And did not Uriah abode in Jerusalem that day, and the morrow? Now when thee had called him, he did eat and drink before thee; and thou made him drunk: and at even he went out to lie on his bed with the servants of his lord, but went not down to his house." And David's silence remained.

"And did it not come to pass in the morning, that thee wrote a letter to Joab, and sent it by the hand of Uriah? And thou wrote in the letter, saying, 'Set ye Uriah in the forefront of the hottest battle, and retire ye from him, that he may be smitten, and die.' And did it not come to pass, when Joab observed the city, that he assigned Uriah unto a place where he knew that valiant men were.?Then the men of the city went out, and fought with Joab: and there fell some of the people of the servants of David; and Uriah the Hittite died also." And David restrained and remained quiet.

"Did not Joab send and tell thee all the things concerning the war; and charged the messenger to inform thee that they hath made an end of telling the matters of the war unto the king, and if so be that the king's wrath arise. Did ye say unto the messenger, 'Wherefore approached ye so nigh unto the city when ye did fight? knew ye not that they would shoot from the wall? Who smote Abimelech the son of Jerubbesheth? did not a

woman cast a piece of a millstone upon him from the wall, that he died in Thebez? why went ye nigh the wall?' And informed thee did they that thy servant Uriah the Hittite is dead also." And David King held his scalded and scolded tongue.

"And did not messenger go forth, and come and show thee all that Joab had sent him for? For surely the men prevailed against them, and came out unto them into the field, and they were upon them even unto the entering of the gate. And the shooters shot from off the wall upon thy servants; and some of the king's servants be dead, and thy servant Uriah the Hittite is dead also.

"And did thee not saith unto the messenger to say uttno Joab, 'Let not this thing displease thee, for the sword devoureth one as well as another: make thy battle more strong against the city, and overthrow it'? and encourage thou him.

"And when the wife of Uriah heard that Uriah her husband was dead, did she not mourn for her husband? And when the mourning was past, thou sent and fetched her to thy house, and she became thy wife, and bare thee a son. But the thing that David had done displeased the LORD and displeased His only Begotten Son."

And David King pulled himself out of the roiling, boiling river of blood and stood on the embankment, then fell on bended his knee in His name, as every knee should bend in heaven and on earth and under the earth, because God highly exalted Him and gave Him the name that is above every name.

And as His command, with a dig into his haunch, Nessus then reared and with iron hooves kicked David the king back into the roiling, boiling river of blood, and He saith unto David, His father, "I hath come to preach unto the

spirits in prison. As for thee also, by the blood of thy covenant the LORD has sent forth My prisoners out of the pit wherein is no water. Thy sins have erased thy name from My Book of life." And David the king splashed and thrashed, drowning in the river of blood, pleading with his son not to abandon His father.

Then back Nessus turned, and passed the centaur again the ford. ✝

Circle 7 – Ring 2
"The Gnarled Wood of the Suicides"

**OT YET HAD NESSUS REACHED** the other side, when they had put themselves within a wood, that was not marked by any path whatever. Not foliage green, but of a dusky colour, not branches smooth, but gnarled and inter-tangled, not apple-trees were there, but thorns with poison. Such tangled thickets have not, nor so dense, those savage wild beasts, that in hatred hold 'twixt the Pishon and the Gihon and the Chidekel and the Phirat the tilled places of the land of Nod.

There do the hideous Harpies make their nests, who chased the Trojans from the Strophades, with sad announce-ment of impending doom; broad wings have they, and necks and faces human, and feet with claws, and their great bellies fledged. They make laments upon the wondrous trees.

His Mute companion heard on all sides lamentations uttered, and person none beheld he who might make them, whence, utterly bewildered, he stood still. **He** thought that

His companion perhaps might think so many voices issued through those trunks from people who concealed themselves from them; therefore **He** said: **"If thou break off some little spray from any of these trees, the thoughts thou hast will wholly be made vain."** Then stretched the mute forth his hand a little forward, and plucked a branchlet off from a great thorn; and the trunk cried, "Why dost thou mangle me?" After it had become embrowned with blood, it recommenced its cry: "Why dost thou rend me? Hast thou no spirit of pity whatsoever? Men once we were, and now are changed to trees; indeed, thy hand should be more pitiful, even if the souls of serpents we had been."

As out of a green brand, that is on fire at one of the ends, and from the other drips and hisses with the wind that is escaping; so from that splinter issued forth together both words and blood; whereat he let the tip fall, and stood like a man who is afraid. **"Had he been able sooner to believe,"** He made answer, **"O! thou wounded soul, what only in My verses he has seen, not upon thee had he stretched forth his hand; whereas the thing incredible has caused Me to put him to an act which grieveth Me. But tell him who thou wast, so that by way of some amends thy fame he may refresh up in the world, to which he can return."**

And the trunk said: "So thy sweet words allure me, I cannot silent be; and you be vexed not, that I a little to discourse am tempted. When the Philistines fought against Israel; and the men of Israel fled from before the Philistines, and fell down slain in mount Gilboa. And the Philistines followed hard after Saul, and after his sons; and the Philistines slew Jonathan, and Abinadab, and Malchishua, the sons of Saul. And the battle went sore against Saul, and the

He *and* His *mute companion enter the Wood of the Suicides!*

archers hit him, and he was wounded of the archers. Then said Saul unto me, his armourbearer, 'Draw thy sword, and thrust me through therewith; lest these uncircumcised come and abuse me.' But I, the armourbearer, would not; for I was sore afraid. So Saul took a sword, and fell upon it. And when I saw that Saul was dead, I fell likewise on the sword, and died. So Saul died, and his three sons, and all his house died together. And when all the men of Israel that were in the valley saw that they fled, and that Saul and his sons were dead, then they forsook their cities, and fled: and the Philistines came and dwelt in them."

And he waited awhile, and then: **"Since he is silent,"** **He** said to **His** mute companion, "lose not the time, but speak, and question him, if more may please thee." Whence the mute sought to say: "Do thou again inquire concerning what thou thinks't will satisfy me; for I cannot, such pity is in my heart," but could not for he was mute. Therefore **He** recommended: **"So may the man do for thee freely what thy speech implores, Spirit incarcerate, again be pleased to tell us in what way the soul is bound within these knots; and tell us, if thou canst, if any from such members e'er is freed."**

Then blew the trunk amain, and afterward the wind was into such a voice converted: "With brevity shall be replied to you. When the exasperated soul abandons the body whence it rent itself away, Minos consigns it to the seventh abyss. It falls into the forest, and no part is chosen for it; but where Fortune hurls it, there like a grain of spelt it germinates. It springs a sapling, and a forest tree; the Harpies, feeding then upon its leaves, do pain create, and for the pain an outlet. Like others for our spoils shall we return; but not that any one may them revest, for 'tis not just to have what one casts off. Here we shall drag them, and along the dismal

forest our bodies shall suspended be, each to the thorn of his molested shade."

And **His** mute companion became greatly afeared that his own shade had journeyed through six circles of Hades only to be led by **Him** into this gnarled wood and to have his own grain to falleth onto the forest floor to germinate and spring a sapling and then become a forest tree in which the Harpies, feeding then upon his own leaves, shalt pain create, and for the pain an outlet. Looking down at his sandals, he perceived his dirty feet having sunk into the moist soil of the forest floor and the black eyes of the Harpies eying him hungrily; he madly brushed off the soil to see if he had become to sprout into a sapling, when—

—Another trunk, with anguish it turned to look upon **Him** and the knots that were its eyes, lit by fireflies, wept sap from its hollow formed a mouth which spoke unto **Him** and **His** mute companion, "Howbeit the hair on my head had begun to grow again after I was shaven and the lords of the Philistines gathered us together for to offer a great sacrifice unto Dagon their god, and to rejoice: for they said 'Our god hath delivered Samson our enemy into our hand.' And when the people saw me, they praised their god: for they said, 'Our god hath delivered into our hands our enemy, and the destroyer of our country, which slew many of us.' And it came to pass, when their hearts were merry, that they said, 'Call for Samson, that he may make us sport.' And they called for me out of the prison house; and I made them sport: and they set me between the pillars. And I said unto the lad that held him by the hand, 'Suffer me that I may feel the pillars whereupon the house standeth, that I may lean upon them.' Now the house was full of men and women; and all the lords of the Philistines were there; and there were upon the roof about three thousand men and women, that beheld while I

made sport. And I called unto the LORD, and said, 'O! LORD God, remember me, I pray thee, and strengthen me, I pray thee, only this once, O! God, that I may be at once avenged of the Philistines for my two eyes.' And I took hold of the two middle pillars upon which the house stood, and on which it was borne up, of the one with my right hand, and of the other with my left. And I said, 'Let me die with the Philistines'. And I bowed myself with all my might; and the house fell upon the lords, and upon all the people that were therein. So the dead which I slew at my death were more than they which I slew in my life. Then my brethren and all the house of my father came down, and took me, and brought me up, and buried me between Zorah and Eshtaol in the buryingplace of Manoah my father."

And He, in a frenzy of a woodsman staring down a wildlife, tore at the gnarled and mangled truck, pulling free sheets of bark with the crazed madness of a priest in his sacrifice to Molech flaying the skin from the children alive. And the tree bellowed from its hollow and lamented from its branches, the gnarled branches strained in the unbearable pain and clutched and clawed at His shoulders, striping His back with its barbs and thorns, until the soul of the Judge was torn free from its prison within the gnarled wood of the suicides; and the shade of Samson stood before his LORD, knowing now the knowledge that he, like the patriarchs and prophets of the Asphodel Meadow, was now free from the apt agony and poetic punishments of the Pit and would stand before the LORD God of Israel in Paradise as was promised by His coming: and Samson bended his knee in His name, as every knee should bend in heaven and on earth and under the earth, because God highly exalted Him and gave Him the name that is above every name. ✠

Samson commits shameful and sinful suicide by toppling the Philistine temple!

Circle 7 - Ring 3
"The Blasphemies of Betzalel, the Viper"

**T**HEN CAME THEY TO THE CON-fine, where disparted the second round is from the third, and where a horrible form of Justice is beheld. Clearly to manifest these novel things, the mute observed they arrived upon a plain, which from its bed rejecteth every plant; the dolorous forest is a garland to it all round about, as the sad moat to that; there close upon the edge we stayed our feet.

The soil was of an arid and thick sand, not of another fashion made than that which by the feet of Cain once was pressed. Vengeance of God, O! how much oughtest thou by each one to be dreaded, who doth read that which was manifest unto mine eyes! Of naked souls beheld I many herds, who all were weeping very miserably, and over them seemed set a law diverse. Supine upon the ground some folk were lying; and some were sitting all drawn up together, and

others went about continually. Those who were going round were far the more, and those were less who lay down to their torment, but had their tongues more loosed to lamentation.

Over all the sand-waste, with a gradual fall, were raining down dilated flakes of fire, as of the snow on Ararat without a wind. As Titus Flavius Caesar Vespasianus Augustus, in those torrid parts of Israel, shalt behold upon his host flames fall unbroken till they reached the ground when to the turn does he put the Temple of God. Whence he provided with his Legions to trample down the walls, because the vapour better extinguished was while it was single; thus was descending the eternal heat, whereby the sand was set on fire, like tinder beneath the steel, for doubling of the dole. Without repose forever was the dance of miserable hands, now there, now here, shaking away from off them the fresh gleeds.

And the mute looking about the sands saw whom he perceived to be Solomon, son of David, builder of the Temple of God, sitting alone with the flakes of fire raining down upon his head and his feet charred by the burning sand beneath him.

This Solomon was old, that his wives turned away his heart after other gods: and his heart was not perfect with the LORD his God, as was the heart of David his father. For Solomon went after Ashtoreth the Goddess of the Zidonians, and after Milcom the abomination of the Ammonites. And Solomon did evil in the sight of the LORD, and went not fully after the LORD, as did David his father. Then did Solomon build an high place for Chemosh, the abomination of Moab, in the hill that is before Jerusalem, and for Molech, the abomination of the children of Ammon. And Solomon glorified Topheth, which is in the valley of the

children of Hinnom, that he might offer his son or his daughter to the brass idol Molech, by worshipping its idol through immense offerings of fire which heated the idol to a glow and then, "O! woe!", did Solomon take his sons and his daughters from the cradle of their mothers and laid the babe in the cradle of the arms of the idol. And did Solomon watch as the generous heat did scorch and sear the flesh of his children, crackling and charring of their flesh was a foul sound, and the stench of the sacrifice that arose to the heights of heaven:

"O! woe!", did the LORD God of Israel lament, "Thou shalt not let any of thy seed pass through the fire to Molech, neither shalt thou profane the name of thy God: I AM the LORD." And the ignited cries of the children placed upon the cradle of the arms of the altar of the idol were a chorus of agony and anguish that arose to the heights of heaven, "O! woe!", did the LORD lament, "Whosoever he be of the children of Israel, or of the strangers that sojourn in Israel, that giveth any of his seed unto Molech; he shall surely be put to death: the people of the land shall stone him with stones. And I will set my face against that man, and will cut him off from among his people; because he hath given of his seed unto Molech, to defile my sanctuary, and to profane my holy name. And if the people of the land do any ways hide their eyes from the man, when he giveth of his seed unto Molech, and kill him not: Then I will set My face against that man, and against his family, and will cut him off, and all that go a whoring after him, to commit whoredom with Molech, from among their people."

And there wandered the sands Betzalel, certain Pharisee circumcised the eighth day, of the stock of Israel, of

King Solomon sacrificing his children to Molech!

the tribe of Benjamin, an Hebrew of the Hebrews; as touching the law, a Pharisee, the son of a Pharisee: of the hope and resurrection of the dead he called in question, who had besought him to dine with **Him**: and **He** had gone in, and sat down to meat. And when Betzalel saw it, he marvelled that **He** had not first washed before dinner.

And **He** had said unto him, **"Now do ye Pharisees make clean the outside of the cup and the platter; but your inward part is full of ravening and wickedness. Ye fools, did not he that made that which is without make that which is within also? But rather give alms of such things as ye have; and, behold, all things are clean unto you.**

And as **He** said these things unto them, the Pharisees and the Sadducees began to urge **Him** vehemently, and to provoke **Him** to speak of many things. For those of them that had died before others of their generation had fulfilled His own prophecy: **"Ye know that after two days is the feast of the passover, and the Son of man is betrayed to be crucified."**

And **He** reminded them, all of the Pharisees and Sadducees, of a parable: **"The kingdom of heaven is like unto a certain king, which made a marriage for his son, and sent forth his servants to call them that were bidden to the wedding: and they would not come. Again, he sent forth other servants, saying, 'Tell them which are bidden, Behold, I have prepared my dinner: my oxen and my fatlings are killed, and all things are ready: come unto the marriage.' But they made light of it, and went their ways, one to his farm, another to his merchandise: and the remnant took his servants, and entreated them spitefully, and slew them. But when the king heard thereof,**

he was wroth: and he sent forth his armies, and destroyed those murderers, and burned up their city.

"Then saith he to his servants, 'The wedding is ready, but they which were bidden were not worthy. Go ye therefore into the highways, and as many as ye shall find, bid to the marriage.' So those servants went out into the highways, and gathered together all as many as they found, both bad and good: and the wedding was furnished with guests.

"And when the king came in to see the guests, he saw there a man which had not on a wedding garment: and he saith unto him, 'Friend, how camest thou in hither not having a wedding garment?' And he was speechless.

"Then said the king to the servants, 'Bind him hand and foot, and take him away, and cast him into outer darkness, there shall be weeping and gnashing of teeth.'

"For many are called, but few are chosen."

And as He spake to Betzalel and his generation of vipers, the Pharisees and the Sadducees from across the centuries that came across the third ring of the seventh circle when they heard the Christ had come unto them: "The scribes and the Pharisees sit in Moses' seat: all therefore whatsoever they bid you observe, that observe and do; but do not ye after their works: for they say, and do not. For they bind heavy burdens and grievous to be borne, and lay them on men's shoulders; but they themselves will not move them with one of their fingers.

"But all their works they do for to be seen of men: they make broad their phylacteries, and enlarge the borders of their garments, and love the uppermost rooms at feasts, and the chief seats in the synagogues, and greetings in the markets, and to be called of men, 'Rabbi,

Rabbi.'

"But be not ye called 'Rabbi': for one is your Master, even Christ; and all ye are brethren. And call no man your 'father' upon the earth: for one is your Father, which is in heaven. Neither be ye called masters: for one is your Master, even Christ. But he that is greatest among you shall be your servant. And whosoever shall exalt himself shall be abased; and he that shall humble himself shall be exalted.

"But woe! unto you, scribes and Pharisees, hypocrites! for ye shut up the kingdom of heaven against men: for ye neither go in yourselves, neither suffer ye them that are entering to go in.

"Woe! unto you, scribes and Pharisees, hypocrites! for ye devour widows' houses, and for a pretence make long prayer: therefore ye shall receive the greater damnation.

"Woe! unto you, scribes and Pharisees, hypocrites! for ye compass sea and land to make one proselyte, and when he is made, ye make him twofold more the child of hell than yourselves. Woe unto you, ye blind guides, which say, whosoever shall swear by the temple, it is nothing; but whosoever shall swear by the gold of the temple, he is a debtor! Ye fools and blind: for whether is greater, the gold, or the temple that sanctifieth the gold? And, whosoever shall swear by the altar, it is nothing; but whosoever sweareth by the gift that is upon it, he is guilty. Ye fools and blind: for whether is greater, the gift, or the altar that sanctifieth the gift? Whoso therefore shall swear by the altar, sweareth by it, and by all things thereon. And whoso shall swear by the temple, sweareth by it, and by him that dwelleth therein. And he that shall

The generation of Vipers dream and scheme against Him!

swear by heaven, sweareth by the throne of God, and by him that sitteth thereon.

"Woe! unto you, scribes and Pharisees, hypocrites! for ye pay tithe of mint and anise and cummin, and have omitted the weightier matters of the law, judgment, mercy, and faith: these ought ye to have done, and not to leave the other undone. Ye blind guides, which strain at a gnat, and swallow a camel.

"Woe! unto you, scribes and Pharisees, hypocrites! for ye make clean the outside of the cup and of the platter, but within they are full of extortion and excess. Thou blind Pharisee, cleanse first that which is within the cup and platter, that the outside of them may be clean also.

"Woe! unto you, scribes and Pharisees, hypocrites! for ye are like unto whited sepulchres, which indeed appear beautiful outward, but are within full of dead men's bones, and of all uncleanness. Even so ye also outwardly appear righteous unto men, but within ye are full of hypocrisy and iniquity.

"Woe! unto you, scribes and Pharisees, hypocrites! because ye build the tombs of the prophets, and garnish the sepulchres of the righteous, and say, If we had been in the days of our fathers, we would not have been partakers with them in the blood of the prophets. Wherefore ye be witnesses unto yourselves, that ye are the children of them which killed the prophets. Fill ye up then the measure of your fathers.

"Ye serpents, ye generation of vipers, how can ye escape the damnation of hell? Wherefore, behold, I send unto you prophets, and wise men, and scribes: and some of them ye shall kill and crucify; and some of them shall ye scourge in your synagogues, and persecute them from city to city: that upon you may come all the righteous

blood shed upon the earth, from the blood of righteous Abel unto the blood of Zacharias son of Barachias, whom ye slew between the temple and the altar. Verily I say unto you, All these things shall come upon this generation.

"O! Jerusalem, Jerusalem, thou that killest the prophets, and stonest them which are sent unto thee, how often would I have gathered thy children together, even as a hen gathereth her chickens under her wings, and ye would not! Behold, your house is left unto you desolate. For I say unto you, Ye shall not see Me henceforth, till ye shall say, Blessed is he that cometh in the name of the Lord."

And all of the Pharisees and Sadducees from across the centuries, who all suffered all of the apt agony and poetic punishments, when they heard these things, were filled with wrath, and rose up, and thrust **Him** out of the shade of the synagogue and led **Him** unto the brow of a hill, over which precipice the eighth circle of Hades could be seen below, and far below the mysterious inky depths of the ninth circle could not be seen. They sought to cast **Him** and **His** mute companion down headlong, but instead of passing through the midst of them to go **Him** way, **He** and **His** mute companion fell down headlong into the depths. ✞

Circle 9
"The Icy Lake of the Unholy Trinity"

THE LORD GAVE HIS ANGELS charge over **Him**, to keep **Him** in all **His** ways. They bore **Him** up in their hands, lest thou dash **He** foot against a stone. **He** shalt tread upon the lion and adder: the young lion and the dragon shalt **He** trample under feet.

When Gabriel and Michael and the hosts of Heaven caught **Him** and **His** mute companion as they were hurled off of the precipice of the third round of the seventh circle and they descended down within the darksome well, far out of reach of the Malebolge, wholly of stone and of an iron colour, as is the circle that around it turns. Right in the middle of the field malign there yawns a well exceeding wide and deep, of which its place the structure will recount. Round, then, is that enclosure which remains between the well and foot of the high, hard bank, and has distinct in valleys ten its bottom. As where for the protection of the walls many and many moats surround the castles, the part

82

in which they are a figure forms, just such an image those presented there; and as about such strongholds from their gates unto the outer bank are little bridges, so from the precipice's base did crags project, which intersected dikes and moats, unto the well that truncates and collects them.

And the angels abandoned **Him** and **His** mute companion beneath the giant's feet, but lower far, and the mute was scanning still the lofty wall, he heard it said to him: "Look how thou steppest! Take heed thou do not trample with thy feet the heads of the tired, miserable brothers!" Whereat he turned himself round, and saw before him and underfoot a lake, that from the frost the semblance had of glass, and not of water.

And as to croak the frog doth place himself with muzzle out of water,– when is dreaming of gleaning oftentimes the peasant-girl,– livid, as far down as where shame appears, were the disconsolate shades within the ice, setting their teeth unto the note of storks. Each one his countenance held downward bent; from mouth the cold, from eyes the doleful heart among them witness of itself procures. When round about him somewhat he had looked, he downward turned him, and saw two so close, the hair upon their heads together mingled. They bent their necks, and when to him their faces they had lifted, their eyes, which first were only moist within, gushed o'er the eyelids, and the frost congealed the tears between, and locked them up again. Clamp never bound together wood with wood so strongly; whereat they, like two he-goats, butted together, so much wrath o'ercame them.

And one, who had by reason of the cold lost both his ears, still with his visage downward, said: "Knowest I not the knowledge that my brother could die! A tiller of the earth was I! Not a keeper of sheep! The beasts of the field and the

beasts of the forest die, but not man! Never once was it known in the knowledge of good and evil that came from the fruit thereof that tree that a man could die!

"And whence the **LORD God** sent Father and Mother forth from the garden of Eden, to till the ground from whence Father was taken. So **He** drove out Father; and **He** placed at the east of the garden of Eden Cherubims, and a flaming sword which turned every way, to keep the way of the tree of life.

"And Father knew Mother his wife; and she conceived, and bare me, and said, 'I have gotten a man from the **LORD**.' And she again bare my brother Abel. And Abel was a keeper of sheep, but I was a tiller of the ground. And in process of time it came to pass, that I brought of the fruit of the ground an offering unto the **LORD**. And Abel, he also brought of the firstlings of his flock and of the fat thereof. And the **LORD** had respect unto Abel and to his offering: but unto me and to his offering he had not respect. And I was very wroth, and his countenance fell. And the **LORD** said unto me, '**Why art thou wroth? and why is thy countenance fallen? If thou doest well, shalt thou not be accepted? and if thou doest not well, sin lieth at the door. And unto thee shall be his desire, and thou shalt rule over him.**' And I talked with Abel my brother: and it came to pass, when we were in the field, that I rose up against Abel my brother, and struck him upon the head with a large stone. And the **LORD** said unto me, '**Where is Abel thy brother?**' And said I, 'I know not: am I my brother's keeper?' And **He** said, '**What hast thou done? the voice of thy brother's blood crieth unto Me from the ground. And now art thou cursed from the earth, which hath opened her mouth to receive thy brother's blood from thy hand; When thou tillest the ground, it shall not henceforth**

yield unto thee her strength; a fugitive and a vagabond shalt thou be in the earth."

"And I said unto the LORD, 'My punishment is
greater than I can bear. Behold, Thou hast driven me
out this day from the face of the earth; and from Thy
face shall I be hid; and I shall be a fugitive and a vagabond
in the earth; and it shall come to pass, that every one that
findeth me shall slay me.'

"And the LORD said unto me, 'Therefore whosoever
slayeth Cain, vengeance shall be taken on him sevenfold.'
And the LORD set a mark upon me, lest any finding me
should kill me. And I went out from the presence of the
LORD and that of Father and Mother, and dwelt in the
land of Nod, on the east of Eden."

" 'Vexilla Regis prodeunt Inferni' Towards us; therefore look in front of thee," the Master of the mute companion said, "if thou discernest him." As, when there
breathes a heavy fog, or when their hemisphere is darkening
into night, appears far off a mill the wind is turning, heth-
ought that such a building then he saw; and, for the wind,
the mute drew himself behind his Guide, because there was
no other shelter.

There where the shades were wholly covered up, and
glimmered through like unto straws in glass. Some prone
are lying, others stand erect, this with the head, and that
one with the soles; another, bow-like, face to feet inverts.
When in advance so far we had proceeded, that it his Guide
pleased to show to him the creature who once had the
beauteous semblance, He from before the mute moved and
made him stop, saying: "Behold Dis, and behold the place
where thou with fortitude must arm thyself." How frozen
he became and powerless then, because even he could speak
all language would be insufficient.

The Emperor of the kingdom dolorous from his mid-breast forth issued from the ice; and better with a Titan compared than do the Titans with those arms of his; consider now how great must be that whole, which unto such a part conforms itself. Were he as fair once, as he now is foul, and lifted up his brow against his **Maker**, well may proceed from him all tribulation.

O!, what a marvel it appeared to the mute companion, when he beheld three faces on his head! The one in front, and that vermilion was; two were the others, that were joined with this above the middle part of either shoulder, and they were joined together at the crest; and the right-hand one seemed 'twixt white and yellow; the left was such to look upon as those who come from where the Nile falls valley-ward. Underneath each came forth two mighty wings, such as befitting were so great a bird; sails of the sea henever saw so large. No feathers had they, but as of a bat their fashion was; and he was waving them, so that three winds proceeded forth therefrom.

Thereby Cocytus wholly was congealed.

With six eyes did he weep, and down three chins trickled the tear-drops and the bloody drivel. At every mouth he with his teeth was crunching a sinner, in the manner of a brake, so that he had two of them tormented thus.

And **He,** having been tempted by a shade of Dis in the form of an old man, relished the circumstance to saith unto Dis, the great dragon, that old serpent, called the Devil, and Satan, which deceiveth the whole world, that his fate had been sealed when he rebelled against the **LORD God of Israel**. And **He** wrote, in proud mockery of **His Father's** Commandments the laws that would govern Satan, the god of the world to blind the minds of them which believe not,

Dis, also called the great dragon, that old serpent, which is the Devil, and Satan, and **He** *bound him a thousand years in the icy depths of the Inferno!*

lest the light of the glorious gospel of Christ, who is the image of God, should shine unto them:

I. "O! Satan, thou shalt blaspheme the Lord with thy every word and thy every breath.

II. O! Satan, thou shalt deceive the whole of the world, as god of this world, having blinded the minds of them which believe not, lest the light of the glorious gospel of Christ, who is the image of God, should shine unto them; and only shalt the true believer shalt truly believe.

III. O! Satan, thou shalt cloud of minds of man to believe I exist not and shalt thee make nation upon nation believe God exists not.

IV. O! Satan, thou shall dishonour thy Father in Heaven and His Son, the light of the world: he that followeth me shall not walk in darkness, but shall have the light of life.

V. O! Satan, thou shalt steal from them their faith in His only begotten Son, whom He gave that whosoever believeth in Me should not perish, but have everlasting life.

VI. O! Satan, thou shalt attempt to murder spirit of men and their souls, who putteth on the whole armour of God, that they may be able to withstand thee in the evil day, and having done all, to stand. They stand therefore, having their loins girt about with truth, and having on the breastplate of rightcousness; and their feet shod with the preparation of the gospel of peace; above all, taking the shield of faith, wherewith they shall be able to quench all of thy fiery darts of the wicked. And take the helmet of salvation, and the sword of the Spirit, which is the word of God.

VII. O! Satan, thou shalt deceive False Prophets, making them believe they hear the Word of God or the voices of the Angels of the Hierarchy of Heaven.

VIII. O! Satan, thou shalt covet the throne of Heaven, and the faith of them who believed in Me and the Father.

IX. O! Satan, thou shalt believe thee are God."

And the Guide of the mute companion saith, "There are two, who head downward are; the one who hangs from the black jowl is Brutus; see how he writhes himself, and speaks no word. And the other, who so stalwart seems, is Cassius. But night is reascending, and 'tis time that we depart, for we have seen the whole."

And He turned to His mute companion and clasped him round the neck and saith, "There is a third unholy mouth reserved for the betrayer of the LORD." And the mute companion struggled to speak, but could not for wild and mongrel dogs had eaten his tongue in the final moments of his life after he had lashed a rope to the strongest bough of a tree and hanged himself. His neck broke not as he flung himself down and he convulsed and strained under the strangling of the rope. He clutched and clawed at his neck, his face scratched to the very bone, the flesh of his cheeks hung in ribbons and his blood cascaded down his chest and back. And the bough of the tree broke and he did fall headlong. Took he did his dagger from his sash and he cut upon his gut and his bowels gushed out and verily a mangy mongrel feasted upon his viscera and flapped his blood, her pups yipping and tugging on a length of his innards, growling and quarrelling over the choicest scraps including his tongue.

"The soul that shall reside there in the third mouth

shalt have the greatest pain," the Guide said, "is thee, Judas Iscariot; with head thy inside, thy legs without.

"Unto every one of us is given grace according to the measure of the gift of Christ. Wherefore the LORD God saith, 'When he ascended up on high, he led captivity captive, and gave gifts unto men.' Now that I shalt ascend, what is it but that I also descended first into the lower parts of the earth? I that descended is the same also shalt ascend up far above all heavens, that I might fill all things. But thee, Judas Iscariot, must I leaveth here in Hades forever more."

And Judas Iscariot, the mute companion, shook his head in disbelief, the same disbelief that caused him, one of the twelve, to go unto the chief priests, and say unto them, "What will ye give me, and I will deliver him unto you?" and they covenanted with him for thirty pieces of silver; and from that time he sought opportunity to betray Him. But now on the icy fields of Cocytus, he feared his Guide all the more. With his eyes wide, his stride short, he stepped further onto the glass that was ice, the glass beneath him began to crack and his Master reached out His hand and Judas refused to accept it, for surely in Judas' betrayal, should be all the right, because God Himself willed that His Son be delivered up and delivered Him up to death, but verily Dis laughed at the very thought to ascribe the guilt of the crime to God than to transfer the credit for redemption to Judas.[1] And Dis seized Judas and with gluttonous hunger flung him into his own guffawing maw. To Judas now in front the biting was as naught unto the clawing, for sometimes the spine utterly stripped of all the skin remained. ✝

---

1 John Calvin

Epilogue
"His Ascent From His Descent"

ITHIN THE SEPULCHRE, THERE sat a young man, clothed in a long white garment, on the right side of the His Body, wrapped in the linen, who awaited the Lord after Christ descent into the Inferno. He knoweth the journey would be harrowing, but he also possessed the knowledge that He predicted His own death and resurrection when He shewed His disciples that He must go Jerusalem and suffer many things from the elders and chief priests and scribes, and be killed, and on the third day be raised. And as the sun rose that Sabbath, the young man knew that His prophecy would not be for naught, for He would ascend from His descent into the Inferno in fulfilment of the scriptures taken in hand to set forth in order a declaration of those things which are most surely believed among us, even as they delivered them unto us, which from the beginning

were eyewitnesses, and ministers of the **Word**.

The great dragon, that old serpent, called the Devil, and Satan, which deceiveth the whole world: he was cast out into the earth, and his angels were cast out with him, Dis with his hair made a stairway still fixed remaineth as he was before. Upon this side he fell down out of heaven; and all the land, that whilom here emerged, for fear of him made of the sea a veil, and came to our hemisphere; and peradventure to flee from him, what on this side appears left the place vacant here, and back recoiled. A place there is below, from Beelzebub as far receding as the tomb extends, which not by sight is known, but by the sound of a small rivulet, that there descendeth through chasm within the stone, which it has gnawed with course that winds about and slightly falls. Our **Eternal Guide** into that hidden road now entered, to ascend from his descent and—

—**His Body** radiated through the grace of the **Holy Ghost** and vanished. And the young man alone heard our Resurrected **Christ** saith in the emptiness of the sepulchre: "I will extol Thee, O! Lord; for Thou hast lifted Me up, and hast not made My foes to rejoice over Me. O! Lord My God, I cried unto Thee, and Thou hast healed Me. O! Lord, Thou hast brought up My soul from the grave: Thou hast kept Me alive, that I should not go down to the pit. Sing unto the Lord, O! ye saints of His, and give thanks at the remembrance of His holiness. For His anger endureth but a moment; in His favour is life: weeping may endure for a night, but joy cometh in the morning. And in My prosperity I said, I shall never be moved. Lord, by Thy favour Thou hast made My mountain to stand strong: Thou didst hide Thy face, and I was troubled. I cried to Thee, O! Lord; and unto the Lord

He *is bodily resurrected on the third day! And recites the thirtieth Psalm of David!*

I made supplication. What profit is there in My blood, when I go down to the pit? Shall the dust praise thee? shall it declare Thy truth? Hear, O! Lord, and have mercy upon Me: Lord, be Thou My helper. Thou hast turned for Me My mourning into dancing: Thou hast put off My sackcloth, and girded Me with gladness; to the end that My glory may sing praise to Thee, and not be silent. O! Lord My God, I will give thanks unto Thee for ever!" ✞

THE GOSPELS OF BIBLICAL HORROR

TRINITY

Book 1

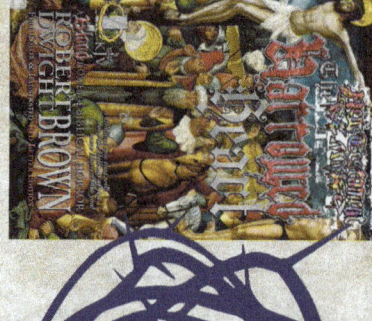

The Harrowed Heart
978-1-931608-48-0
$15.00

Book 2

The First Exorcist / The Harrowing of the Inferno
Special FLIPable Printing
ISBN: 978-1-931608-60-2
$17.00

Book 3

The Machination of Vipers
978-1-931608-71-8
$15.00

Artwork Bibliography

Blake, William, *The Great Red Dragon and the Beast from the Sea*, 1805, National Gallery of Art, Washington D.C.

Blake, William, *The Great Red Dragon and the Woman Clothed with the Sun*, c. 1805-10, National Gallery of Art, Washington D.C.

Blake, William, *The Number of the Beast is 666*, 1805, Rosenbach Museum and Library, Philadelphia

Blake, William, *Whore of Babylon*, 1809, British Museum, London

Botticelli, Sandro *Temptations of Christ*, 1480-82, Sistine Chapel, Vatican City

Bourdon, Sébastien, *King Solomon Sacrificing To The Idols*, 1600's, Lourvre Museum, Paris

daVinci, Leonardo, *The Annunciation of Mary*, c. 1472, Uffizi Gallery, Florence, Italy

Furini, Francesco, *The Birth of Benjamin and the Death of Rachel*, 17th century, Alte Pinakothek, Munich Germany

Josephson, Ernst, *David and Saul*, 1878, Nationalmuseum, Stockholm

Memling, Hans, *The Last Judgment*, c. 1466-73, National Museum, Gdańsk, Gdańsk, Poland

Rembrandt, *Christ in the Storm on the Lake of Galilee*, 1878

Rubens, Peter Paul, *Massacre of the Innocents*, 1611-12, Art Gallery of Ontario

Tiepolo, Giovanni Domenico, *Christ and the Woman Taken in Adultery*, c. 1758-59 Lourvre Museum, Paris

Tissot, James, *Jesus Tempted in the Wilderness*, c. 1886-94 Brooklyn Museum, New York

Bosch, Hieronymous, Follower of, *The Harrowing of Hell*, Indianapolis Museum of Art, Indianapolis, Indiana

Bosch, Hieronymous, Follower of, *Christ In Limbo*, c. 1500-1599, Philadelphia Museum of Art, Philadelphia, Pennsylvania

Botticelli, Sandro, *Map of Hell*, c. 1480-90

Bouguereau, William-Adolphe, *Dante and Virgil*, 1850, Musée d'Orsay, Paris France

Buoneri , Francesco, called Cecco del Caravaggi, *The Resurrection*, Art Institute of Chicago, Illinois

Doré, Gustave, *Dante and Virgil before Pier della Vigna*

Doré, Gustave, *Satan*

Dürer, Albrecht *Christ in Limbo*, 1511, Germanisches Nationalmuseum, Nuremberg, Germany

Gérôme, Jean-Léo, *Bethsabée*, 1889

Matsys, Jan, *Lot and his daughters*, 1565, Royal Museums of Fine Arts of Belgium, Brussels, Belgium

Kharon, Lytovchenko Olexandr *Charon carries souls across the river Styx*, 1861, Russian Museum, St. Petersburg

Tissot, James, *Samson Pulls Down the Pillars*

Rubens, Peter Paul and Jan Brueghel the Elder, *The garden of Eden with the fall of man*, c. 1615, Mauritshuis, The Hague, Netherlands

Tissot, James, *The Pharisees Question Jesus*, c 1886-94 Brooklyn Museum, New York

Valckenborch, Martin van, *Parable of the Wicked Husbandman*, 1580-90, Kunsthistorisches Museum, Vienna, Austria

Artwork Bibliography

Flip book over to continue...

Jesus was crucified, died, and was buried! Then He made a journey in His daunting **Harrowing of the Inferno!**